LOVE SONG

LOVE SONG

•

Wilma Fasano

AVALON BOOKS
NEW YORK

PRINTED IN THE UNITED STATES OF AMERICA
ON ACID-FREE PAPER
BY HADDON CRAFTSMEN, BLOOMSBURG, PENNSYLVANIA

To my husband Jim, with love.
Thank you for spending two months exploring
New Zealand with me.

Prologue

Two men stood on a sidewalk in Bangor, Maine. The sign behind them read H. GALLANT, ACCOUNTANT.

"Thanks, Jon," the older man said as they shook hands. "I feel a lot better about Judy going off like this to New Zealand, now I know you'll keep an eye on her. Although how you're going to manage without her knowing what you're up to, I don't know."

"Trust me, Harold," Jon Brown said. "Remember, I make a living with my imagination. I'll think of something."

He clapped Harold Gallant on the shoulder, then turned and strode off, leaning into the chill November wind.

Chapter One

Jon Brown waited in the Bangor airport. Waited and watched. In the two months since Jon had reluctantly agreed to keep an eye on Judy, Harold and Marian Gallant had successfully overseen Judy's itinerary so that it matched his own. He'd thought out his strategy. It might change when he met the woman, but for now he'd depend on the very human trait of curiosity to keep her from running away or calling the police.

He recognized her as soon as she entered the room, a slight young woman about five-foot-four, with an intense expression. An abundance of curly red-gold hair, styled in a pixie cut, covered her head. Her gray-green eyes were large, wide-set in an oval face. Her mouth was wide and generous, her nose small and pert. There was a dusting of pale freckles that the New Zealand summer would change, but now her fair complexion was clear, almost translucent.

That last might well be a result of her illness, as might the fact that she was obviously underweight.

Those things, and a general fragility, were all that indicated she was not in robust health. She was dressed in loose-fitting denim jeans with matching jacket. Under the jacket, she wore a white T-shirt. He nodded his approval.

She was much more attractive than the tomboy he remembered from twelve years ago when she was thirteen with freckles and braces and sharp knees and elbows. Hopefully, she wouldn't have any recollection of him.

When Judy came through the door of the Bangor airport, she saw a young man half-lounging against a wall, guarding a suiting, a large wheeled suitcase, a tote bag, and a guitar case. He'd probably be about thirty, tall and muscular and wearing, of all things in January, faded denim cutoffs which looked as if they'd been hacked with pinking shears from worn-out jeans. His white, short-sleeved cotton-knit shirt appeared to have seen better days.

On his head he wore a fishing hat, old and green and battered. A bright-red fishing lure pinned one side of the brim to the crown, in the fashion of Australian army hats.

The hat partially covered his mass of dark curly hair. He had the tanned outdoor look of a man who skied a lot or took winter vacations on tropical beaches. Laugh lines crinkled at the corners of his mouth and eyes. Under their dark straight brows, his eyes were as blue as a tropical sky.

For some reason, he was staring at her.

Whoops. She'd been staring at him. Not a good idea. She turned away and struggled with two overstuffed suitcases, large tote bag, camera, and purse. When she sneaked one last peek she discovered his piercing blue eyes resting on her. Before you could say "kiwi," the stranger lazily uncurled from the wall and in two strides was at her side.

"Here," he said, "let me help you with those."

He picked up the three suitcases effortlessly, and shepherded her to the end of the shortest line. He then set the bags down around her, went back for his own, and returned to stand behind her.

"You're not with anyone? Did you come on the bus or something?"

"No," Judy said. "A friend brought me, but he dropped me at the door and then went to park the car. His name's Walter."

The stranger scowled.

As if it were any of his business.

She remembered her manners. "Thank you for helping me out. It really was quite a struggle." She put out her hand. "I'm Judy Gallant from Bangor, and I'm on my way to New Zealand. Well," she added, "not really from Bangor. A small town near Bangor, but it's where my parents live and everybody's heard of it."

He held her hand rather than shaking it. "Hi, Judy. I'm Jon Brown, spelled J-O-N. Plain Jon Brown from Boston." He continued to hold her hand. When the line moved, he nudged the pile of bags ahead with his feet.

"Next, please." With a start Judy saw that she was

at the head of the line, and that this fascinating, badly dressed stranger still clutched her hand.

She snatched it away, and, somewhat flustered, retrieved her ticket and passport from her purse and showed them to the woman behind the counter. Jon Brown placed the two largest suitcases on the scales as he looked down at her with a lazy smile.

She saw Walter coming through the door.

"Oh," she blurted as she took her boarding pass and luggage tickets and picked up her tote bag, "there's my friend now. Well, Jon, it was nice meeting you. Thanks so much. Have a nice trip. Good-bye."

"Not necessarily," he said with an indolent grin as he put his own cases on the scale and produced his passport.

Now what on earth did he mean by that? She turned her attention to meeting Walter. They walked past car rental booths, past a travel agency, and rode up an escalator.

Walter cupped a proprietary hand under her left elbow and steered her toward the coffee shop. He picked up coffees for them both, and they walked into the back part, their steps muffled in the carpet.

Judy slipped into a booth, with her back to the door. Walter sat down facing her. Her eyes were on Walter, but her mind was on the handsome stranger.

She brought her attention back to Walter as she heard him say her name with some irritation.

"Oh," she said, "sorry. What was that?" and her concentration drifted off again.

Walter was nice, but ordinary. He certainly wasn't

the romantic hero of her dreams. His eyes were blue, but neither piercing nor steely. Instead of unruly dark curls, he had medium brown hair, neatly combed. He was good-looking, she supposed, and, as her mother kept pointing out, romantic heroes rarely existed in real life, and when they did, they usually didn't make good husbands. Walter would be a successful banker. He would make some lucky woman, not her she hoped, a good husband.

Walter waved his hand, pendulum-like, in front of her eyes. She blinked.

"Snap out of it, Judy. What's wrong? You're a million miles away."

She forced herself to give him her attention. "Sorry again. Guess I was just dreaming of my trip."

A quivering of hairs on the nape of her neck told her that Jon Brown had entered the room. Walter sat facing him.

"There's the fellow you were talking to when I came in," he said in a low voice. "The guy that looks like a beach bum."

Judy resisted turning her head.

"Just a stranger who helped me with my bags. He seems very nice."

"He's gone," Walter said. He added, "You're too trusting, Judy. Sometime you're going to run into trouble taking up with strangers."

"Oh, quit being so stuffy. All he did was help me with my bags in the middle of a crowded airport." Her face turned red. "Now why don't we just drop it?" She fought against turning around to see if he had really gone.

Walter reached out and patted Judy's hand. "You're really set on this trip, aren't you, Judy? You think it's wise, especially considering your health."

She exhaled in disgust. "Don't be silly. I just had a touch of environmental illness."

"A touch? You missed almost all the last two months of school."

"Environmental illness, Walter. Environmental illness. It was the school that made me sick. My classroom. Carpets and mold. Some of the kids were sick too, but not as badly. And the maintenance people are going through the school and removing carpets. Besides that, I'm being transferred to a new school in the fall. I'll be fine." She wanted to pull her hand away, but that would be rude.

"Uh, I have some vacation time coming. Would it be okay if I came out for a couple of weeks, say in March?"

She didn't want him to, but there seemed no easy way to tell him that.

"It's a long way," she said, choosing her words carefully, "and it's a lot of money for so short a time." She hesitated, then plunged on. "You realize that we're just friends. If you come, it's with that understanding—we're just friends. Okay? If you'll accept that, I'd love to see you."

She squeezed his hand, feeling like a hypocrite. "My parents have a list of places and approximate dates I'll be picking up mail. Write and let me know."

* * *

An hour later, Judy stood in the crowded aisle of the airplane, struggling to lift her tote bag into the overhead racks.

"Here," said a familiar voice, "let me help you with that."

She looked up. It was Jon Brown, complete with curly hair and piercing blue eyes. She shouldn't have been surprised. After all, he'd been in the same line at the check-in counter, but still she blurted out the words, "What are you doing here?"

His eyes held hers. "Flying. Why do people generally check their bags with airlines?" He took her arm. "And now, maybe we'd better get out of the aisle so all these nice people can get by."

Resentment boiled in Judy. *Nice people indeed.* "Don't patronize me," she said.

He ignored her and continued to take charge. Before she knew it, her jacket and camera were in the overhead rack along with Jon's hat, the heavy tote bag was under the seat, and she next to the window. Jon Brown's long body was stretched out in the seat beside her. His legs and arms, even the backs of his fingers, were covered with dark curly hair. Judy's eyes were drawn to the mat of black chest hair at the neckline of his cotton shirt.

She was both annoyed and disturbed. Maybe Walter was right and she was too trusting. But of course Jon having the next seat was coincidence. It had to be. People didn't change their seats once they were on the plane. He'd probably just come down from Boston on business and now he was going back. Then why hadn't he taken a direct flight to Boston rather than one through Newark?

He turned to her with a disarming smile. "Come on, Judy," he chided. "Quit looking at me in such a prickly fashion. After all, do I really look like Jack the Ripper?"

She looked at him. "No," she said, "no, you don't. But then, I don't suppose Jack the Ripper looked much like Jack the Ripper either."

"Touché." He added, "But we're in a plane together, there are all sorts of people here with us, and we're going to be seatmates. So why don't we just relax and get to know each other?"

How she could possibly relax with him so disturbingly close eluded her, but she could hardly tell him that, so she nodded.

She shivered with nervous anticipation as the jet thundered down the runway and rose into the air. Jon put his right arm loosely around her and squeezed her shoulder reassuringly.

"Wonderful, isn't it?" he said. "No matter how often I do it, I never find it boring."

She relaxed then, a bit. He seemed really nice.

Almost unconsciously, she began telling him about herself, forgetting her natural shyness, confiding in this stranger on this magic airplane bound for romance, adventure, and New Zealand.

"I teach sixth grade," she said, then continued telling him what had happened. She'd become allergic to the molds in her classroom. As the term went on it had become worse and worse. She sneezed nonstop and the medication she took for the sneezing made her drowsy. Then she began to lose her energy.

Her doctor made her take sick leave for the last six weeks before Christmas and told her she'd be better off to get a leave of absence for the spring term and get back to her usual robust health. " 'Lots of sunshine, good food, and outdoor exercise,' " she quoted. "So I said that I could get those things as well in New Zealand as in Maine, so here I am. He objected for a few minutes, my parents objected a lot more, and then they gave up, bought my ticket as a Christmas gift, and helped me plan my itinerary."

She even found herself telling him about the writing she hoped to do. After all, she'd never see him again after Newark. She was a romantic at heart, she admitted, and she intended to write romances. As a child she'd loved fairy tales, as a teenager cried through *Jane Eyre* and *Wuthering Heights*, and as an English major adored romantic poetry. During the next six months, she intended to get back to glowing health, as well as seeing New Zealand and writing a romance novel.

"Mmm," he murmured, "need any help with the research?"

"Oh." She smiled at him. "Do you know a lot about New Zealand?"

"You're extremely naive. I wasn't talking about New Zealand."

"Oh!" The nerve. She drew back sharply and shrugged his arm off, then jerked her head away abruptly and crowded as close to the window as she could get within the cramped confines of the airline seat and her seat belt. What sort of nut had she fallen in with? Well, if she wanted to write romances, she was already getting material.

She grabbed at that explanation. After all, she'd told him about the writing. Maybe he was entering into the spirit of the thing and setting up a scenario for her. At least, that was the most comfortable theory.

She said frostily, "I suppose that I told you about the romance, and you're entertaining me with a bit of role-playing. That's the kindest explanation I can think of anyway."

He smiled. "If that makes you happy, let's go with it." His smile was disarming. "So why don't we make up and be friends? It'll make the rest of the trip a lot more tolerable. I'm sorry if I upset you."

He didn't look a bit sorry, but she supposed the job of a writer was to examine as many strange pieces of humanity as possible. That was the approach to take— think of him as a lesson in character study. Besides, the "rest of the trip" shouldn't be more than half an hour.

"All right." She turned to him and held out her hand. "Pax."

"Pax," he replied as he took her hand but held on.

Easy, Judy, she reminded herself. *You're the scientist of romantic fiction, and he's the lab animal, remember?*

Well, he was certainly an animal and a very magnetic one at that. She didn't withdraw her hand, and she supposed all the sensations that went through her as he stroked each separate and individual finger might be useful to a writer of romantic fiction.

The arrival of the plane at Newark interrupted Judy's thoughts. She tried to think more about her trip and less about Jon Brown, who seemed to be at her elbow at every turn.

"Don't you have somewhere to go?" she said.

"Ah, didn't I remember to tell you? I'm going to New Zealand."

Funny. Going from Boston to New Zealand through Bangor and Newark seemed a strange route, but there appeared to be little about Jon Brown that wasn't strange. Maybe he was joking.

Not so. When she boarded her plane for Los Angeles, Jon Brown was in the next seat. It did, really and truly, seem that he was going to New Zealand, and that by fate, or luck, or good management on his part, he was going to continue sitting by her. She was excited, but more than a little apprehensive. Who was Jon Brown? By what unlikely stroke of coincidence did he have the seat next to hers on every leg of the trip? Why did her feelings about him flip-flop between attraction and annoyance?

Between watching the cities come and go and eating the plastic lunches and saying, "No, thank you, I don't drink," she found that the flight to Los Angeles went by very fast.

There were nearly three hours to spend in the Los

Angeles airport, and, from habit, Judy headed for the nearest row of seats.

Jon took her arm. "No, you don't. You're going to be sitting on the plane so long, you'll be lucky if your feet don't swell up like balloons. So while we're here, we're hiking."

"Hiking? In the airport?"

"Yep. Didn't your doctor say to exercise?"

"Outdoor exercise."

"Considering that's out of the question right now, I think this is better than nothing. Twenty minutes for a mile, then a short rest, then another mile. Come on."

"Huh. You're suggesting we walk six miles in the airport corridors while we're waiting for our plane?"

"You'd be better off in a restaurant eating greasy hamburgers? Now, come on. If you feel tired after the first three miles, we'll quit."

He reached out and took her tote bag and camera, hanging them over one shoulder with his own bag, apparently without effort. He reached out his free hand to take hers.

Oh, well. No matter how weird he was, he couldn't hurt her in the Los Angeles airport.

She gave a shiver of anticipation and left her hand in his.

Off they went, up and down the halls, hand in hand, for twenty minutes. It was sort of fun, although he set a terribly brisk pace. She didn't feel as tired as she'd thought she would. And, yes, she had no doubt that her doctor would approve.

"Okay," Jon said at the end of twenty minutes. "Fifteen minutes' rest." He pulled her over to the line of seats and deposited the bags. They sat down.

In almost no time, he said, "Recess over," and they started off again.

"Why are you doing this?" she asked.

"So you won't get to Auckland with swollen feet and jet lag. True, it would be better to hike later, but we won't have time or space anywhere else, so let's get on with it."

As they walked he sang in a rich clear voice, but softly, apparently for her ears alone.

*"I'll woo you in Auckland, I'll wed you in
  Christchurch
I'll chase you all over the New Zealand coast.
Your eyes are like emeralds, your cheeks are like
  roses,
But your lips like wild honey are what I'd like most."*

Judy pulled her hand from his grasp, and stood and glared at him, arms akimbo. "And just what's all that about?"

"Oh," he said. "Just a little ditty I've worked up. I always sing to the women I pick up in airports." His eyes mocked her. "Why? Did you think it meant you?"

"Huh." She blew out a breath in disgust as she looked at him. He stepped toward her and framed her face with his hands.

"Maybe it did at that," he said softly. Then, before she could react, he bent his head until his lips hovered over hers, touched hers, kissed hers. Her lips tingled. Her chin tingled. She closed her eyes and sighed and tingled.

He drew back as if burned. "Sorry about that, Judy. Let's keep walking." He jammed his hands into his pockets and strode down the corridors of Los Angeles airport.

When the plane left Los Angeles, it was almost dark. Jon told Judy to nap as much as possible.

"After all, you don't want to spend the day you arrive sleeping, or you'll have a dreadful job adjusting to New Zealand time."

"You've traveled a lot?"

"A fair amount."

Maybe he was a rich eccentric.

She'd tolerate him—strictly in the interests of literary research, of course. And because she couldn't do anything about it without making a major scene. Anyway, the advice about napping seemed good. Jon didn't pester her any longer, and when she surfaced between catnaps to find his arm around her and her head on his shoulder, it seemed so comforting that she didn't even bother to pull away.

In a day or so, the plane would land in Auckland. She and Jon would go their separate ways, and she would never see him again. There was surely no great harm in resting her head on his shoulder for now.

After the evening meal, Jon said, "Why don't you go do whatever you do before bedtime, and when you get back, you can lie down with your head against me and I'll cover you with a blanket."

She should object, but the prospect of a comfortable sleep was tempting.

When she returned from the rituals of washing up and brushing her teeth, she saw that Jon had folded one of the airline blankets on her seat and was holding the other.

"Get in," he said, "and curl up as best you can. It won't be great, but it's better than sitting up. I've moved the arm rest between us out of the way, and you can rest your head against me."

He hustled her in by the window, then sat down. She was tempted.

"But what about you?" she asked. "Won't this be terribly uncomfortable for you?"

The familiar gleam was in his eye. "Maybe," he said, "I'm just getting material for a book."

"Oh," she sputtered. "Oh."

"Listen," he said, "if your worst fears are confirmed and I'm an ax-murderer, won't you find it easier to cope if I'm the one who's exhausted, and you're the one who's had the good night's sleep? Now lie down."

She did, and he covered her with the blanket. When she glanced up at him he looked a bit like a cat that has a mouse on hold, but isn't hungry just yet. He began to sing softly, the same song he'd crooned in the airport.

It was comfortable, so very comfortable, so comfortable that she forgot the comparison to the mouse and the hungry cat. Her head lay cradled on his arm, and she could hear the steady beating of his heart, regular as a metronome, lulling her to sleep.

Chapter Two

W hen Judy first glimpsed New Zealand, the morning sun shone on little clouds that romped like fluffy lambs across a gentian sky.

She sat, nose pressed against the window, absorbing every detail as she looked down on the green countryside, divided into farms and fields by hedgerows. The hills were more rugged than she'd expected, and there were inlets and bays and peninsulas everywhere—a charming jigsaw puzzle of a country.

When the plane landed, she turned to Jon with mingled regret and relief, determined to do the right thing. She held out her hand.

"Thanks for your company, Jon," she said. "It was nice meeting you. It's been a most, uh . . ." She fumbled for an appropriate word.

"*Interesting,*" he said. "*Interesting* is the word you're hunting for. And after that, I think you were about to come up with *good-bye*. But don't say good-bye too fast. That didn't work in Bangor, and I don't think it's going to work here either. You're not rid of me yet."

Before she recovered from her surprise enough to answer, they were off the plane and into the airport. It was like the countryside, cool and green and soothing. Jon was at her elbow, eyes intense and blue and disturbing. They were whisked through luggage carousels and customs with hardly a pause. Almost at once she was at the tourism desk being directed to the rental company's courtesy car, and Jon was still behind her.

"Mind if I come with you? I want to find out about renting a camper."

Excitement surged through her. She still had him for another half hour. Besides, he was pushing the cart with her luggage.

"Whatever you want," she said.

At the rental agency, Jon disappeared into an office. Judy walked to the parking lot, then stood disconsolately beside a red compact car, keys in hand, wondering what on earth to do next. She loved the car, but somehow when she'd been halfway around the world making arrangements, she hadn't really taken in the enormity of having to drive it on the wrong side of the road all over this foreign country.

Earlier, she'd turned to the nice young woman at the desk for reassurance, asking if North Americans ever got into trouble driving, hoping to be told they hadn't lost one yet, but the woman had smiled cheerfully and said, "Oh, yes. That's what most of our accidents are—tourists getting confused when they're trying to drive on the left-hand side of the road."

Judy was still working on her courage when she heard Jon's voice. "Want me to drive this thing to the hotel for you?"

"Jon!"

He reached for the keys and smiled lazily. "Look, if you're really worried about my being Jack the Ripper, we can go back in. I'll give them my name and social security number and tell them I'm with you, so that when your battered and mutilated body is found lying in a ditch, the police will know just where to look."

"Oh, don't be silly," she said shortly, hoping he didn't realize how closely he'd touched on her fears. "But I thought you were getting a camper?"

"Won't be ready until Wednesday. Now, how about it? Which are you less afraid of? Me or that car?"

"You," she said, relieved, and handed him the keys before sliding into the passenger seat.

"Now, where to?"

She named the hotel.

"What a coincidence—just where I'm staying. If they have any rooms left," he added with a grin as he started the car and drove it out onto the busy highway.

She stuck her chin out with determination. "You didn't try to get a camper for today, did you?"

He looked at her sideways. "Do you wish I'd got a camper for today?"

She reddened as she watched cars rush by madly, all on the wrong side of the road. "No," she muttered.

In a very short time they were at the hotel. When she'd checked in, he carried her bags to her room and told her to change into comfortable clothes and meet him in the lobby in thirty minutes.

"I thought I might sleep for a couple of hours," she said.

"Not a great idea. You had a good sleep on the plane, and if you stay awake today and go to bed at the normal time tonight, you'll be all set. Otherwise your body will try to keep you on Bangor time for days. So why don't we meet here in half an hour? Take a shower, and then dress in shorts and a comfortable top."

He left to see about a room for himself. She wasn't sure whether she hoped he got it or not. She supposed she'd have to come to terms with the car at some point, but hopefully not today.

There was no reason to unpack everything. She could afford this hotel for only one night. She placed her suitcase on the extra bed. Shorts, he'd said—shorts and a comfortable top. She dug into her suitcase and found white walking shorts, not too badly rumpled, and a plain blue cotton T-shirt. Then she peeled off the jeans and top she'd lived in for the last two days.

The shower felt good, and so did the shorts and the clean shirt. She was still rummaging for fresh socks when she heard a tap on the door.

"Come on, slowpoke. I'm tired of waiting. You're not asleep, are you?"

She padded to the door in her bare feet and let him in. He'd had a shower too. Droplets of water still clung to his hair. Khaki shorts and a short-sleeved khaki shirt, open at the neck, had replaced the cutoffs.

Judy's tote was opened on the bed. Jon glanced at it, pulled out a pair of white sports socks, and handed them to her.

When she'd finished tying her shoes, he walked with her through the lobby and out into the parking lot where her little red car sat, eyeing her, she imagined, reproachfully. Jon still had the keys.

"I thought," he said, "that we might drive around the city a bit, with you as a passenger, and then find some place in the country for a late lunch/afternoon tea. Then if you have the courage, and if we can find a quiet residential area somewhere, maybe you can have a short driving lesson."

She nodded. She wasn't completely comfortable about Jon, but as yet she feared the red car more. And since that kiss in Los Angeles, he'd been very well behaved. Still, she must stop letting him boss her around and must stop being flustered whenever he was near. Ms. Cool. That's what she'd aim for now. Cool and sophisticated. She smiled and climbed into the passenger seat.

When they reached a cozy tearoom on a hilltop, Jon guided her up to the viewing platform on the roof. They looked down on the city of Auckland and its harbor spread below them.

"It's lovely," she said. "I can't believe I'm really here. I've dreamed of it so long that I couldn't quite believe it would really and truly ever happen. Not until the plane touched down this morning."

She summoned up her courage, took a deep breath, and went on, "And you've been wonderful to me, Jon. I'm afraid I was a bit leery of you at first, but I've decided I was imagining things. I—I'm sorry I mistrusted you, and I'm sorry I was so stubborn. I know that after tomorrow morning, I'll never see you again, so none of this matters."

He turned and, for a moment, glanced out over the city, then looked down at her. He was laughing at her, actually laughing. "Maybe. Maybe not."

He grinned at her in a lazy way that made her heart turn cartwheels and made her forget her anger. "And now," he said, "why don't we go on down and have tea?"

They had mutton rolls and something delectable that was mostly whipped cream wrapped in lacy brittle caramel, followed by strong hot tea.

When they got back to Auckland Jon found a quiet cul-de-sac and traded places with her in the car. He was very patient, as if she were a beginning driver, but he made her do turns at intersections again and again. When she began to tire, he took over and drove back to the hotel.

"The hotel has a buffet on Sunday nights," he said. "I suppose we may as well go?"

"Only if I pay my own way." Afternoon tea was one thing, but a full dinner was something else. Women of the new millenium took care of themselves. Jon Brown, whoever he was, needn't think she was anything but independent.

His eyes twinkled. "Whatever makes you happy."

She sighed. "How should I dress?"

"Not too fancy. I'm staying as I am. Maybe you could change your shorts for a simple skirt."

She put on a navy blue skirt and a pair of flat-heeled white sandals. She paid for her ticket somewhat defiantly, but after a good meal and two helpings of trifle with whipped cream, she began to mellow. A two-man band, piano and guitar, played lazy, old-fashioned music, and by the time Jon suggested spending the next day exploring beaches north of the city, she was so relaxed that she agreed.

She was in bed, drowsy and content, when she heard the silvery notes of a guitar outside her window. It sounded as if the guitarist were in the pool area. He played melodies rather than just strumming chords. Vaguely she wondered if she should get up and look out the window, but the fatigue of the trip and the time change were catching up to her, so she stayed where she was, listening dreamily to the musician. It was probably the guitarist from the dining room having a bit of practice.

The musician began to sing. Judy took in a sharp breath. She recognized the rich baritone, louder than the times she'd heard it before. Of course. There'd been a guitar case in his luggage. She listened more alertly, and then she got out of bed and went to the window. Jon sat in one of the poolside chairs. He must have sensed the movement at her window, for he looked up, smiled, and waved, then continued singing.

He sang some of the sentimental songs they'd heard earlier that night in the dining room, and then some romantic ballads. She was almost hypnotized. The warm velvet night, the stars so close she felt she could reach out and touch them, the guitarist—once more in his Australian hat—so good-looking that a lump came into her throat, the love songs and the mellow music of the guitar. She almost loved him. In that setting she supposed she'd have almost loved anyone. He looked at her again, and strummed a few familiar bars of the song he'd first sung to her.

She couldn't be angry. It was too beautiful, too romantic. Who was Jon Brown? A movie star? A singer? He could be. Whoever Jon Brown was, he'd never be boring. She smiled to herself as she went back to bed to dream of romantic heroes and storybook endings.

Jon sat in the dining room drinking coffee while he waited for Judy.

He'd made a fool of himself when he'd kissed her in the Los Angeles airport, even if it had been a gentle and innocent kiss. At least that's what he'd intended when he'd kissed her. Then, when she'd closed her eyes and sighed softly, rockets had lit up the airport. If he didn't get himself under control, this might prove to be a very long trip.

He made even more of a fool of himself whenever he sang that wretched song. Telling her that he always made up songs for women in airports was especially stupid. But the lyrics kept popping into his head every time he looked at Judy. That was no excuse for singing them to her.

All he'd accomplish with the singing and the bullying would be to get her upset, and he didn't blame her. What would happen if she became frightened of him and left? How could he fulfill his promise then? At least, hopefully, he'd piqued her curiosity to where she'd hang around to see what happened next.

Never mind taking care of Judy. It seemed as if Jon Brown was the one he had to watch.

Finally he ordered breakfast.

When Judy arrived, he was on his third cup of coffee and surrounded by dirty dishes. He stood up and seated her and got her coffee, then sat back to keep her company while she nibbled her way through a couple of pieces of toast. He looked at her neat tailored pants and shirt.

"You probably should wear shorts and a casual top, with your swimsuit underneath for hassle-free changing if we want to explore beaches."

She frowned. "Do you realize you've spent this whole trip telling me how to dress?"

He met her scowl with an open grin. "This is just the third time," he said. "And have I been wrong?" She had to smile back at him as she admitted, "No," and added, "I'll change as soon as I've eaten. Then I have to check out."

"Check out?"

"Yes. I can't afford hotels—any hotels. I'm going to buy a tent and camp. Why? What difference does it make to you?"

He shrugged. "Never mind. Don't worry about it. Just go change."

She threw down some money for her coffee and toast and left the room.

Of course. He'd known she intended to spend only one night in Auckland. The golden beaches weren't on her itinerary either. It didn't matter if they didn't follow the planned route for the next few days. Bayside was the first place where they had reservations.

Judy returned, wearing emerald-green shorts with a matching T-shirt and casual canvas sandals. She carried a tote bag with the end of a beach towel trailing from it.

"I left my other bags in the lobby," she said.

Jon carried her suitcases to the car while Judy checked out.

"Are you sure you've thought all this out?" he asked as they drove north.

"Yes," she said. "I'm on a tight budget. I can buy a tent and sleeping bag for the price of a night or two in a hotel and stay in the campgrounds."

"Ah, yes," he remarked dryly, "and you plan to fast for six months, or are you also buying a kitchen range, a full set of dishes and pots and pans, and spices?"

"I've done my homework," she retorted. "The campgrounds all have kitchens, and I can buy a lot of bread and cheese and fruit and things like that."

"All right," he said. "That makes sense. As long as you stick to the nutrition program your doctor advised."

"That isn't really your business. I wouldn't have

told you, except that I assumed after Newark, I'd never see you again."

"Never assume anything," he said.

He stopped at a sporting goods store and helped her pick out a light tent, a suitable sleeping bag, a flashlight, and a compact kit of camping dishes with a frying pan that converted into a plate and with everything fitting into something else. When the time came to pay, Jon wandered over to the fishing rods and left her on her own. She wouldn't appreciate his supervision at this point and would only be insulted, rightfully so, if he offered to pay.

They stowed the camping gear into the car.

As Jon drove away from Auckland, Judy watched the scenery and thought of the appalling amount she'd just put on her credit card. Before long, Jon swung off the main highway and onto rural roads that followed the coast. The roads wound through, and over, hills. Sheep, cattle, and the most splendid horses that Judy had ever seen grazed in the pastures. The farmhouses were new and prosperous looking.

Jon turned into a cove, and parked beside a long, deserted white sand beach.

"Never mind the towels," he said. "We'll just walk here and swim a little farther up the road."

When they arrived at the beach, they took off their shoes and walked at the water's edge. The beach stretched for miles. White breakers rolled in across the turquoise water. Jon reached out for Judy's hand, and she gave it to him.

"Happy?"

"Oh, yes," she said. "Yes."

They walked in silence. Judy breathed in the salt air, scuffed her feet through the hard ridges of the beach, and watched the aura that spread out around her foot when she stepped on wet sand. The tide came in warm and lovely, and once, when they wandered too far into the water, an incoming wave caught them on the bottoms of their shorts. They scrambled for dry ground, laughing, still hand in hand.

As long as he doesn't spoil this by kissing me again.

She didn't mind the songs, although surely they weren't sincere. After all, she'd just met the man. Either they were an elaborate joke, or else he was amusing himself by giving her material for her book. Occasionally, nagging thoughts still plagued her. She wondered if he might be a criminal, and if it was wise to get too close. What were his intentions?

He hadn't been at all secretive. They'd been seen together everywhere. The car rental and the airlines had his name, and both had treated him with considerable respect. He'd shown his passport on two different occasions when she was present. No, she concluded, she was probably quite safe. At the very worst, he might be a married man out for a good time, and she could handle that by saying no.

They returned to the car and drove on to a protected cove of golden sand and clear salt water. A number of local people were there. Kids built sandcastles while doting mothers watched and read. Older kids threw out a fishnet while their black Lab rushed about barking furiously at every passing seagull. A group of women sat in swimsuits under a tree and played bridge. There was a lot of beach, and it wasn't crowded.

The bridge players bid a small slam in diamonds as Jon and Judy walked past and found the shade of a distant tree where they placed their towels and shoes and suntan lotion. Jon stepped out of his cutoffs and pulled off his cotton top. Judy looked at him, bronzed and muscular in blue swim trunks. Maybe he was an athlete, a hockey or football player. He certainly had the build.

"Coming for a swim?"

Somewhat self-consciously she took off her shorts and top, and stood revealed in a classic swimsuit of emerald green.

"Hmm," Jon said. "Very nice."

He reached for her hand, and they ran out into the sun-warm water, first splashing and then swimming. He swam superbly. His strong arms cut the water effortlessly and the muscles of his back moved smooth as silk.

There were advantages to having been a tomboy. Judy matched him stroke for stroke in the buoyant, clear salt water. When she tired, as happened frequently these days, she turned on her back and floated with her eyes closed and let the golden sun beat down on her.

All too soon, they swam back to shore, and then waded the final distance hand in hand. Droplets of water glistened on Jon's head and on the black hair of his chest and arms and legs. What woman could resist him? But she had to. Until she knew more, she had to.

She spread her towel and prepared to lounge in the sun.

Jon shook his head. "Sunscreen first, or with that fair skin you'll look like a Maine lobster in no time."

She spread the lotion carefully over her face, the front of her body, her arms, and legs.

"Here," he said, taking the bottle from her. "Lie down, and I'll do your back."

She stretched out, facedown, the sun blazing down upon her. Jon's strong capable hands smoothed lotion upon her back. It was lovely. She wanted to purr. She wanted this to go on forever. She shouldn't feel this way. Walter could well be right about her being too trusting. Jon was for all intents and purposes still a total stranger.

There was some comfort in the fact that they were on a public beach. The women still played bridge, the kids still built sandcastles, and their mothers still read. She was quite safe, she assured herself.

His hands roamed over her back and shoulders, working the lotion in, rubbing and stroking in large circles. She relaxed. Eventually he stopped, spread out his towel, and lay facedown, close to her. He turned toward her.

"You're beautiful," he murmured, "so beautiful." His face was very close to hers. He brought up one hand and ran his forefinger gently across her eyebrows. "Do you know something? Your eyebrows and eyelashes are golden. I didn't notice that before. Golden. Eyes like emeralds, set in gold."

"Oh," she said, "I guess my mascara must have washed off when I was swimming. I know they're pale. That's why I always wear mascara."

"No, Judy, not pale—golden. They're very unusual and very lovely. Please don't ever wear mascara again. It would be a shame for you to look like a copy of everybody else."

She should have told him it was none of his business what she looked like, but she was too contented to protest. He wriggled a little closer to her, and shifted his hand to the back of her head. He moved just enough for his lips to touch her face and gently kissed her.

Before she knew what was happening, she'd wound her hands in his hair, and pulled his mouth to hers, delighting in the rasp of his wiry chest hair against her bare shoulder.

He drew away first and grinned at her.

"Judy, darlin', I can't believe you did that."

Neither could she. She'd suffered a moment of temporary insanity. But that was it, the end. The absolute end. She wouldn't let Jon Brown close enough to touch her again.

Jon turned away.

Judy wasn't sure when she'd been so embarrassed. She heard the splash as he hit the water, and got up hurriedly, scrambling into her shorts and top. She felt that the whole world must be staring at her, scandalized. But no, the women were intent on their bridge game. The black dog knew he could catch a seagull if he only persisted. Nobody seemed aware that Judy existed, never mind that she'd brazenly kissed a stranger upon this golden beach.

Jon came back, dried off, and stretched out on his towel, completely dispassionate. She stood, shifting around uncomfortably, unable to look at him.

"Sit down," he said. "There's nothing to be embarrassed about. It was just a kiss. It's not your fault you're so lovely. Just relax. I won't hurt you."

She sat down gingerly, careful not to touch him, but he reached out and took her hand, idly twisting her fingers in his own.

He said, "I have to go back. I have some meetings in Auckland tomorrow that I can't avoid."

"Why didn't you say something? We shouldn't have done this. We shouldn't have come so far. Or I could have come on my own."

"That's exactly why I didn't say anything."

"Oh," she said. "I should have realized. You didn't bring any bags and you had the camper booked."

"It's okay. I wouldn't have missed today for anything. Now here's what I'm going to do. You don't have to come back—that would leave you to drive in the city again when I get the camper. I'll book you into a motel for the next two nights. I'll catch a bus into Auckland and come back with the camper Wednesday morning. Then I'll give you some more driving lessons."

"But my tent—"

"Never mind your tent. You can start using it after

I get back with the camper." He looked at her. "Judy, in your whole life, have you ever put up a tent by yourself?"

"Of course I have. I was a Girl Scout."

"Oh. Well, you aren't ready to drive your car yet. It was my idea, and I'll pay if that's bothering you."

"No." She shook her head. "The budget isn't that tight. I'll pay myself."

"Fine. Now don't move until I get back. Explore the town, walk down to the beaches, whatever you want. But don't touch that car. Understand?"

She nodded. She should jump to her feet and rant and scream and tell him he'd better not give her any more orders. She didn't do any of those things.

The sun was warm, and the sand was warm, and she was still sated with the memory of his kisses and the feel of his hands over her warm back. The embarrassment had gone. It was, after all, as he had said, just a simple kiss.

It was mid-afternoon when Judy settled into the motel Jon had booked for her. It was a small apartment, complete with stove and refrigerator, pots and pans and dishes—everything but the food. She was hungry. Lunch had disappeared in a flurry of sand and surf and kissing, and she'd had only toast for breakfast.

She walked downtown, wandering through gift shops, buying postcards and stamps. Then she turned her attention to the food. Bread, cheese, a half-pound of butter, and a bit of fruit would more than see her through dinner and breakfast. She'd deal with tomorrow when it came.

Tomorrow she'd spend at the beach, but tonight she'd stay in, have a leisurely dinner with several cups of tea (makings supplied with the room), write postcards, watch some television, and wash the sand and salt out of her hair. It sounded lovely and relaxing.

And it was. Except for the postcards. The one to her parents presented a problem. *"I met this wonderful man on the plane, and we've been together ever since, even though I don't know who he is or what he does and I don't know whether I'll ever see him again."* Not likely. Her dad would be out on the next plane to take her home, regardless of how old she was. He'd use her recent illness as an excuse.

She remembered that this was only her second day in New Zealand.

She'd known Jon exactly three days—four if you went by the calendar, but Saturday had disappeared at the International Date Line. It seemed a lifetime. She forced her attention back to the postcard, and decided the only way out was to pretend that she and the red car were getting along beautifully, and that she was having a perfectly wonderful time ambling around New Zealand completely on her own.

Probably in another day or two that would be the truth.

She went to bed early, after carefully checking that all doors and windows were securely locked. Maybe tomorrow she'd take her notebook to the beach and get started on the book. As she drifted off to sleep, she dreamed of the hero, a hero with crisp dark curls and eyes as blue as the hot New Zealand sky.

About one, she awoke. She wasn't sure why but decided she'd probably gone to bed too early. Then she remembered that if she were in Bangor she'd be getting up about now. Whatever the reason, she tossed about in bed unable to sleep, and her mind ran like a caged squirrel on a treadmill, worrying to death every morbid thought she could muster up, and she had no shortage of morbid thoughts.

What was she doing here by herself, halfway around the world? This unfamiliar country, so warm and comfortable by day, suddenly became ominous. She heard eerie sounds outside, footsteps on the roof, and fingernails prying in the edges of the door.

The motel proprietors knew she was alone, and they had keys for her door. Could she be sure they were as homey and friendly as they'd appeared, or did they supplement their incomes by selling the passports that had belonged to the American tourists whose bodies were now beneath the kitchen garden?

The branch of a pohutuwaka tree outside her room scraped against a window, sending her into a paroxysm of fear.

A new squirrel leaped onto the treadmill of her mind. This man she'd taken up with? She must be mad. Who was he anyway? He hadn't told her what he did or why he was in New Zealand. Jon Brown? The name Jon Brown was as anonymous as John Doe.

Chapter Three

Eventually, as Judy lay in bed feeding her fears, she ran out of new ideas, so she recycled the old ones with further embellishments. One thing she knew—she had to get away from Jon while she still could. He'd probably exaggerated her driving problems. Everybody else did it. Regardless of what the nice young woman at the counter had said about tourists and accidents, rental agencies wouldn't go on renting cars to North Americans if all they got back were crumpled heaps of metal with dead bodies tangled into them.

Maybe she should just go back to the airport and go home. But no, even in her frightened imagining, her pride wouldn't allow that—everyone smirking and saying, "I told you so." Then her mother would make her chicken soup because she'd been sick, and her Aunt Lucinda would try to feed her spinach and sigh for the good old days when a mustard plaster would fix anything.

No. This was the chance of a lifetime, to have her

dream vacation while she convalesced from her brush with environmental illness.

But she would leave here in the morning and gradually make her way to Bayside, a village in the Bay of Islands where she had a campground reservation in another three days. As soon as the office opened, she would check out and leave. After all, who was Jon Brown to decide where she would stay and for how long?

In the morning, Judy awoke to glorious sunshine. The pohutuwaka tree had reverted to being a mass of beautiful blooms, each looking like a bright-red wire brush. Judy's irrational terror had subsided, but her doubts about Jon remained. Her fears about madness, organized crime, and bigamy were probably greatly exaggerated. At worst, Jon was a womanizer amusing himself. At best, he'd moved in and taken over her life, telling her what to wear, how much makeup to use, where to stay.

"Well, over my dead body, Jon Brown," she declared. "In the space of New Zealand, find me if you can."

Just before she left, in a pointless gesture of defiance—pointless because he would never know—she slathered twice the usual amount of brown mascara on her brows and lashes. Then she eased the red car very carefully out of the parking lot, muttering nonstop to herself, "Keep left. Keep left. Keep left."

She made her way to the main road. Once she got onto it, the threatening highway of her nightmares became an ordinary two-lane paved road with frequent passing lanes. There wasn't enough traffic to be intimidating, and there was no real temptation to cross the center line and drive on the right-hand side.

However, in a few hours she was bone-tired. There was no reason to cover miles of highway every day. She was here to wander around and to write, and, at present, to shake Jon Brown. When she saw a campground sign on the left-hand side of the road, she turned in.

Yes, there was a tent site left in the campground, just one. She was very lucky, the proprietor said. Bookings were heavy this time of year.

She paid for her site and drove the car in. Then she unpacked the tent and looked at the heap of canvas and rods and ropes and pegs strewn on the ground. She reviewed her Girl Scout training from years ago, gritted her teeth, and made the pile of debris into a tent. Lunch was bread and cheese and fruit, her first food since the previous day. Her doctor would not approve.

The tent was hot and the campground crowded, so she took her notebook and walked around until she found a quiet spot in the shade of a tree. She'd toyed with the idea of bringing her computer, but had decided she already had too much luggage.

After she'd settled herself comfortably, she nibbled her pen. Maybe she should start with character sketches. She tried heroes with blond hair and gray eyes, dark hair and brown eyes. The hero with the black curls and piercing blue eyes kept thrusting his image at her, but there was no way she was going to use *him,* so she kept slapping him down.

When she went to bed, she listened to the reassuring family noses in the tents close-packed around her. The restlessness of the previous night had taken its toll, and she awoke only when the heat in the sun-drenched tent made further sleep impossible.

She decided to continue up the coast, but not as far as Bayside. She'd drive a short distance and continue to sightsee and write.

If Jon wanted to find her, he'd probably return to Auckland, and then, eventually, he'd give up. She headed back to the coast. In a few hours, she began to stop at campgrounds. The answers always were, "Sorry, miss, but we're full."

It was still early in the day. Shortly after lunch she began to inquire at motels as well as at campgrounds, but the story was always the same. "Sorry, miss, we're full up. This is our busy season, you know."

The guidebooks had said it was both safe and legal to camp anywhere, but she didn't have quite that much courage.

She came to a decision. She'd go to Bayside. If the campground there had no room, she'd take her tent and, for the one night, pitch it on the beach. The next night, she'd claim her reservation.

Although she hadn't driven far, all the stops and starts and turns had taken their toll. Toward the end, she'd begun to check campgrounds and motels on the right-hand side of the road. She was relieved when a road sign pointing to the right read BAYSIDE. As she drove she saw signs that warned of steep grades. Sure enough, the gravel roads became dustier and steeper with every mile she drove.

She was ready to pull over and pitch her tent any-where, but here "anywhere" on one side seemed to be hundreds of feet down at the bottom of a gorge and on the other side hundreds of feet up at the top of a cliff. The road between appeared to get narrower and narrower as the cliffs became higher and the chasms deeper. There were dead animals on the road, and she was sure she would end up like them. However, there was nowhere to go but straight ahead, with her car as close to the left-hand edge as she dared. The vegeta-tion in the gorges was lush and green, and over every-thing rose the constant singing of the cicadas.

Judy nosed the car around the next sharp turn. There, facing her in the road, was a pickup truck. She swerved her car violently to the right to avoid a col-lision, just as the truck driver swerved to his left for the same purpose. They both hit the brakes. Judy's car slid sideways in the road, and the truck driver, by some marvelous combination of luck and skill, man-aged to stop with about two inches between his truck and the side of the car.

The truck doors opened, and two men got out, big burly unshaven men, shirtless, and in grimy work pants and rubber boots. Judy slammed down the door locks. What should she do now?

The men stood in the road, as if equally unsure of the next move. Then Judy heard a rap on the window, whirled around, and saw Jon's face. Frantically she scrambled to pull the lock up, her earlier imaginary fears forgotten. When Jon opened the door, she darted out to meet him. She knew how ridiculous it was, when her potential accident had turned into a none-vent, but she was frightened. The tensions of the past few days, the difficulties of this back road when she still wasn't ready to drive in New Zealand at all, the narrow escape from a serious accident—it had all built up to an irrational fear.

Jon stepped back and grasped her by the arms. "What's going on here?" he said. "Why are you here? Who are these men?"

She took a deep breath. "We came around the cor-ner at the same time. But they stopped in time. It's all right." She added a bit reluctantly, "But I'm glad to see you, I really am. I'm not sure how I was going to get the car around them."

"You're okay?"

She nodded and smiled weakly at the men standing uncertainly in the road. "I'm sorry I locked myself in," she said. "I know it wasn't your fault, and I should have just got out and apologized."

"That's all right," said one of the men. "I know we're a rough-looking lot."

"No, no. It's not that. It was nothing to do with you. Really. I'm dreadfully sorry, but I'd driven too long, and the campgrounds and motels were all full, and this road got higher and narrower and steeper, and there were dead animals, and cicadas singing, and the ditches were a thousand feet deep, and then I almost had that accident, and I'm as far away from home as it's possible to get." Her voice became higher and shriller. She tried to laugh, ended in a squeak, and she said, "And—and—I'm sorry about everything. I really am. I know I was on the wrong side of the road, and it was all my fault."

"Would you like me to drive your car down into town, miss?" the truck driver asked kindly. "Then you can ride with your friend here."

She felt as if a great load had been lifted from her. "Oh, would you? Really? That's wonderful."

"No," Jon interrupted. "She appreciates the offer, but she can't take it."

She sputtered. She couldn't do it. She couldn't get into that car again and take the wheel and drive over these narrow roads. She turned to Jon.

He spoke gently. "No, Judy. It's like getting back on a horse after you fall off. If you don't take that car into Bayside tonight, you'll never drive in New Zealand again. I can't let you do that to yourself."

The man who'd offered his services broke in, "He's right, miss. I meant well when I offered, but he is right."

She sputtered again. Jon Brown and his arrogant dominating ways. To say nothing of the truck driver agreeing with him. Men all stuck together. That was for sure.

Jon tightened his grip on her shoulder. "It'll be all right, Judy. I'll go ahead of you, slowly, and you can follow me in."

He turned to the men. "If you aren't in a rush, why don't we all have tea first?"

There was a chorus of "Good on ya" and "Right, mate." Judy watched from the side while Jon and the truckers moved vehicles around to get them off the road where she had been sure no "off the road" existed. Then Jon put his arm around her again, and they all walked around the curve. Up ahead was a motor home.

"How did you get here?" Judy asked.

"Well, when I reached the motel and discovered you'd taken off, my only hope was that you'd make for the Bayside campground. So I came straight there by ferry, and when you hadn't booked in yet, I headed out here on the off chance that you'd taken this road. It was a very long shot, but the only hope I had."

Yes, she'd been glad to see him, but why had finding her been so important to him? She'd put her suspicions on hold for now. These two other men were here. It wasn't the time to start a fuss. But she certainly had a few questions for Jon Brown when she got him alone.

They all entered the camper. Jon seated Judy at one side of the table while the truckers took the other. Then he bustled around making tea and setting out biscuits. That done, he sat beside Judy, spooned sugar generously into her cup, poured the tea over it, and gave it to her.

"Drink it."

"But I don't take sugar," she protested.

"You are today. Now drink it."

"Bossy, bossy," she muttered under her breath. She

wouldn't have stopped there if it hadn't been for the truckers.

However, the hot, sweet tea gave her an instant shot of energy. Jon massaged her neck and shoulders steadily over the course of the next half hour, sending little prickles of sensations along her nerve-endings. He turned his conscious attention to the two men. The conversations washed over Judy—the price of wool, how the latest government was doing, harness racing. Jon seemed not only interested in but also fairly knowledgeable about all these things. Gradually with Jon's massaging, Judy's tight muscles eased. A pity the easing of muscles came with an acceleration of heartbeat.

Finally Jon turned to her and asked if she were ready.

"Not really," she said. "Do I have to?"

"Yes, you really have to. It'll be all right. Trust me."

Trust him? How had he known where to look for her?

He asked the truckers to direct him while he turned the motor home around in the narrow road, and then it was time. He walked her back to her car and reassured her. "Just follow me. It'll be all right. Stay about thirty feet behind. I'll drive slowly. If I intend to stop, I'll flick my brake lights twice."

She swallowed again and nodded. Before long, the road widened and flattened, and just as they came to the downtown area, he flicked his brakes and stopped. She stopped too and waited as he came back to the car.

"Okay, you did just fine. Pull over and lock up. Once we get the camper set, we'll come back and get the car. The walk will do us good."

Shortly they were at the campground. As soon as Jon had checked in, he backed the vehicle around and parked it as easily as he'd handled her small car. When he finished, they walked back. He was right. The walk was just what she needed. He drove her car to the campground, and pitched her tent. Then he took her into the camper and whipped up an omelet and salad for supper, while she sat at the table and watched him.

The omelet turned out golden and fluffy, full of cheese and tasting of butter. The salad was crisp and fresh.

After the meal, he poured tea for both of them and leaned back.

"All right, my lovely," he said, "it's time we had a talk. I was angry enough to throttle you if I hadn't been so glad you weren't hurt. Now, what's all this about? Why did you leave the motel when I told you not to? Why did you take off with that little car when you knew you weren't ready? What's going on?"

The meal and tea had revived her, and she'd had time to think. She was the one with a right to be angry. She was the one entitled to answers.

"Maybe I'm the one to ask the questions," she said. "What right do you have to be angry? What business of yours is it where I go? Why do you insist on fol-lowing me around? What made you think I'd come toward Bayside? I'd never told you that. Why didn't you go to Auckland or take some other road? Why did you come this way?"

"Would you believe it was just a lucky guess?"

She clenched her hand around the teacup so tightly she expected the plastic to crack.

"Not really. But what else could it be?"

"Well, almost everybody does the Bay of Islands. This is a logical place to go to for that." But brash, arrogant Jon Brown couldn't quite meet her eyes as he said it.

"Of course. And I suppose if I believe that, you just happen to have this bridge you'd love to sell me. Last question. Just who are you?" She snorted. "Jon Brown? Sure you are. Every crook in the world is either Joe Smith or Jon Brown. Which are you?"

"I *am* Jon Brown," he said. He held his cup in both hands as he leaned his elbows on the table. "I'm not a madman, I'm not a criminal, I don't have a wife, and I hold a very responsible and respectable position."

"Doing what? Why don't you just tell me who you really are?"

He paused. "Let's just say I have my reasons."

"Right. But you're not going to share those with me. Why the big secret? Why did you want to find me anyway? What's going on here?"

"I'm taking care of you," he said abruptly.

She scrambled up from the table. "What do you mean, 'taking care of me'? By whose orders? For what reason? For how long?"

"For all the time you're in New Zealand."

"I've a good notion to go to the police and get a restraining order put on you."

"Why don't you do that? If it will make you feel better, we'll go to the police station together, I'll show the police my credentials, and they can assure you that you're unlikely to come to harm at my hands."

"You'll show them these credentials in their office, of course, while I wait out front."

"Of course."

"Why? Just tell me why."

He looked at a loss. *Bully for him.*

"Go on. Tell me."

"Well," he said finally, "well, I guess I'm just attracted to you."

"Yeah, right. That's the usual way to show attraction. To refuse to tell the woman who you are. Walter might not have your drop-dead good looks, but at least I know his real name, and I know what he works at, and that he hasn't ever been in jail. I don't know any of those things about you."

"Please, Judy. Trust me."

What could she do? He'd fed her and taught her how to drive and just rescued her from the very worst moment of her life. He'd said the police would vouch for him if she asked. Maybe he was bluffing, but, just the same, she couldn't do it. After the way he'd rescued her and protected her, how could she drag him to the police station?

She had to smile.

"Then we can go on like this a bit longer?"

She nodded. Just the same, she'd watch herself a lot more carefully around Jon Brown in the future.

"You've had a bad day, and you're tired. Why don't you stay here, and I'll take the tent?"

"No," she said. "I couldn't. I just couldn't do that."

"Why not?"

"I couldn't. It wouldn't be right." There was no way she'd let herself get more obligated than she already was. Besides, if she was in the tent and anybody bothered her, Jon Brown or anyone else, the whole campground would hear her scream.

"All right. Your choice. Now run along to bed. I'll be around to serenade you in a while."

She was in bed dozing when she heard the first notes of the guitar. He seemed to be sitting on the hillside, and for a time he plucked out the melodies of the old romantic ballads that she loved. Then he started to sing, softly at first. She listened as she snuggled drowsily in her sleeping bag. Soon there were other voices. A crowd was gathering, and, as requests came in, the romantic ballads were followed by traditional campfire songs and by modern songs. There appeared to be some Australians in the crowd, for the rousing strains of "Waltzing Matilda" rang through the campground.

It sounded like such fun that she wanted to join them. She could, she knew. All she had to do was put on her jeans and a shirt and wander out, and Jon would say, "Oh, hi!" and reach out and pull her down to sit beside him on the grass. It would be so easy, and she wanted to, but she just couldn't.

Yes, she was shy, but it wasn't just that, she told herself. If she went out now, Jon would think she was under his spell to the point that she couldn't stay away from him.

Eventually the party wound down, and the campers drifted away. When the singing stopped and Jon went back to just playing, she assumed that he was alone again. He played a while longer, strummed a few chords, and began to sing her that familiar song.

Her melancholy mood lifted, replaced by a warm glow. Maybe she was a stupid fool for not sending him away, but would any woman in the whole world be able to resist him?

He was attracted to her, he'd said. And here he was, following her around New Zealand, serenading her every night underneath her window—well, actually outside her tent door—just like a troubadour of old. It was exciting and romantic, and it was happening to her, Judy Gallant from Bangor, Maine. She drifted off to sleep, smiling to herself, dreaming of her knight in shining armor, her chivalrous hero, the man with the piercing blue eyes and the laugh lines around his eyes and mouth—plain Jon Brown from Boston.

The morning after Judy arrived in Bayside, she sat in front of her tent doing her best with a stale cheese sandwich. She heard Jon whistling as he came along the path.

"Aha," he said, "eating well with the help of the campground kitchens, I see. The benefits of doing one's homework, I presume?" She resisted the temptation to throw the stale sandwich at his head. He continued cheerfully, "We can go on a cruise at a quarter after ten, so I'll come around for you at about nine-thirty if that's okay, and we'll saunter downtown at our leisure. Uh, my treat."

She started to protest.

"Don't worry," he said, "I'll manage to make it deductible. Better get moving. It's almost nine now." He turned and left, hands in pockets, battered Australian hat on his head, still whistling.

She spent a few minutes playing the mental game of "Who is Jon Brown?" Hockey player was probably eliminated. It wasn't likely a hockey player could write off a cruise in New Zealand. The part about getting moving was right on. She threw the rest of the sandwich at a hopeful seagull, collected some coins, and ran for a shower.

When she returned to the tent, she hurried into her swimsuit and pulled on her emerald shorts and top. She was still fastening her canvas sandals when she heard Jon's whistle. Quickly, she popped her purse and a towel into her tote bag and went to meet him. When he held out his hand, she placed hers in it.

"Did you hear me serenading you last night?"

"Yes." She swallowed. "The sing-along sounded like fun."

He gave her a shrewd look. "You should have dressed and come down. Why didn't you? Are you shy?"

"No," she said, "I just didn't feel like it." *So there.* Jon Brown wasn't going to push all her buttons.

They reached the wharf, and boarded the waiting launch. It was spacious and cheerful with a bright blue carpet and polished wooden walls. Jon and Judy looked around briefly, then climbed to the upper deck.

The captain's commentary was both entertaining and informative. This run had originated for the purpose of collecting cream from the farms around the bay, and even now it was to some degree a working boat, delivering mail, groceries, milk, and newspapers to island residents, and picking up outgoing mail. Judy listened as she stood by Jon at the rail, the summer breeze drying her curls, which were still damp from her hurried shower.

As the boat cruised, the captain pointed out sights of interest. The bird on the right that looked like a huge seagull with a yellow head was a diving gannet. It could dive at speeds of up to ninety miles per hour when it spied a tasty fish below the surface.

The boat stopped at islands and delivered things just as the captain had said. At some, packages were exchanged from the wharf. At one the goods went out and back on a rope and pulley that looked like a clothesline. At another a kid with a yellow dog rowed out to meet the boat. Later, the launch snuggled up to a yacht while the stewardess handed over the daily paper. A restaurant on one of the islands was the designated lunch spot. The noon stop was a lengthy one.

"I didn't get tickets for lunch," Jon said. "I thought we could spend our time in better ways than sitting in a restaurant with a hundred other tourists."

Judy's stomach growled. She'd eaten nothing since last night but a few bites of a stale cheese sandwich.

Jon continued, "I packed us a lunch. I thought we'd hike up the hill to the lookout, and eat there. If we have extra time, we can swim." He nodded at the clear green water and added as an afterthought, "You brought a suit?"

"Yes," she said. "I have it on."

The boat eased up to the wharf. Jon and Judy picked up their bags, and made their way down the ladder and off the boat. In company with the few other passengers who bypassed the restaurant, they went through a gate, over a stile, and up a steep path.

All around, clusters of sheep grazed or lay down on the short-cropped grass. The path led to the ridge of a long hill which, on either side, sloped downward to the sea. In all directions, emerald islands nestled in turquoise waters.

Jon grinned. "Isn't this better than a crowded restaurant?"

Judy breathed deeply of the clean salt air. "It is indeed." For now, she'd put her pique behind her. Knowing Jon did make life a lot more fun. To say nothing of the effect he had on her pulse rate.

He led her to a patch of grass on the highest point of land, and they sat down. Jon drew a packet of sandwiches, a thermos of tea, and two cups out of his tote bag.

"Eat hearty, my lovely," he said as he poured her tea.

She was famished. She bit into a sandwich—ham,

tomatoes sliced paper thin, and lettuce. It was good, so good. She ate another, and another, and drank the hot tea. Jon brought out nectarines and paper napkins. Her contentment was complete as she finished the last drop of tea and lay with her head in his lap, gazing over the tranquil scene.

There was time to spare when they got back down the hill, so they had their swim. They struck off into the green waters of the bay.

Suddenly Jon touched her arm. "Look," he said. There in the bay before them, following a glass-bottomed sight-seeing boat, was a school of dolphins, swimming and cavorting and plunging through the water, smiling their enigmatic dolphin smiles.

Chapter Four

It was still mid-afternoon when the cruise boat returned to Bayside. Jon and Judy lingered on the wharf.

"I'd like to take you to dinner, Judy."

She was surprised and began to protest, but he cut her off. "It's just a date, a regular date. I know you're independent, but surely you accept dates. If the fellow who drove you to the Bangor airport asked you out to dinner, you wouldn't need an arbitration board to decide who paid, would you?"

"Well, putting it that way—" She took a deep breath and said with mock formality, "Yes, Jon Brown, sir, I'd be just delighted to be your dinner date. And what time should I be ready, sir?"

He chuckled as he threw his arm around her shoulders and squeezed. "That's better. I'm going to try to get reservations for six or six-thirty on the next island. It's a bit early for dinner out, but we want to take our time and still catch the last ferry. I'll tell you for sure later. Coming back to the campground now?"

"No," she said. "I'd better do some grocery shopping. I'll see you later."

He walked on up the hill while she wandered along the main street of Bayside. More bread and cheese seemed unimaginative, but that's what she ended up with, as well as eggs, fruit, and some canned goods. She put the perishable supplies in the community fridge when she got back to the campground.

She had to do some unpacking. Green shorts wouldn't do for dinner out, although she wondered if Jon planned to appear in denim cutoffs and his Australian hat. He did, good looks and all, seem determined to look like a beach bum, although clean, she had to admit—always clean.

She reached for her big suitcase. She had a summer dress with short sleeves and a scoop neckline. It was white, printed with small blue flowers. The full skirt fell halfway down her calf, and a wide belt of the same material cinched her waist. She felt very feminine when she wore it. Yes, there it was. She took it to the laundry room and ironed it, and then had a leisurely shower, washing her hair carefully and afterward blow-drying it.

When she finished dressing, she dragged her sleeping bag under the little window in the back of the tent, rolled it up, and sat on it. She pulled out her makeup kit and examined her face in the mirror. Golden lashes, he'd said. He loved her golden lashes. They still looked like straw to her, but if he liked her golden lashes, so be it. Tonight she would dress to please him.

She peered at herself again. The New Zealand sun

obviously loved her freckles. The pale dusting had turned into a brown mass. Well, Jon Brown was so fond of natural, maybe he'd like the freckles too. In the end, she limited herself to eye makeup, just enough to bring out the green lights in her eyes.

Finally, she inventoried her shoes. High heels were probably not suitable for clambering around wharves and ferries, but she had a pair of flat sandals, the ones she had worn to dinner in Auckland, white, with thin, thin straps. She slipped them on and was ready.

She took her rolled-up sleeping bag outside because of the excessive heat in the tent and sat on it, reading while she waited. Jon's whistle warned her of his approach. She hurriedly stood up, throwing the bag and the book inside the tent.

He had cast off the cutoffs and the Australian hat, and was wearing dark dress pants with a white shirt, short-sleeved and open at the neck. He looked at her with approval. "You're lovely, Judy," he said.

She muttered something about sun and freckles, and he said, "I like freckles. They're natural."

She burst into laughter. He raised his brows, and she took his hand as she said, "Don't worry about it. It's just a private joke."

Then she added, smiling up at him, "I've had such a good time today, Jon. The best day of all."

"It's not over yet, darlin'," he said softly as they started down the hill.

The restaurant Jon had chosen had stained-glass windows, fishnets hanging from the ceiling, cool carpets, and polished wooden tables and chairs. There were candles and fresh flowers on all the tables. Classical music played softly in the background. After the tent, and the campgrounds, and the little red car, which always seemed so disappointed in her, to Judy it was a glimpse of heaven. She sank gratefully onto a cushioned chair. Jon seated himself opposite her.

"Like it?"

"Oh, yes. It's been so long. Well, not really, but it seems so long." She hadn't gone out socially since the previous October, when her school began to affect her health. "It seems just like a date at home—a real date."

"It is a real date. Just a date—no strings attached."

The waitress brought them sherries while they looked at the menu. Judy didn't normally drink, but she sipped her sherry slowly. It was, after all, part of the atmosphere. She read the menu and wavered between lamb and fish and venison, but came back to lamb. You couldn't be in New Zealand and not have lamb. It would be like traveling in Maine and not having lobster and clam chowder.

The food was delicious. They lingered over the appetizers, the main course, the dessert, the coffee. Jon was charming. He talked about previous travels in New Zealand, and about the other places he'd been, and about books and poetry. He asked her about herself and her teaching career.

He was a fascinating, sophisticated companion, but he didn't tell her anything more about himself. A couple of times she tried to guide the conversation around to his job and his life, but it wasn't any use. Tonight was too perfect to spoil by making an issue of it.

All the same, a chill crept up her spine. If he had nothing to hide, why didn't he just tell her?

Suddenly he looked at his watch. "Come on. We seem to have been here for hours. Better leave if we're going to make that ferry."

They made it, and she didn't object when he sat with his arm around her. It was nice. He was nice. The whole evening was a lovely, rosy dream.

The ferry docked at Bayside. Jon and Judy stood on the wharf, hand in hand, looking out to sea, reluctant to end the magic. The other passengers went ashore, and they were alone. The full moon hung in the tropical sky, and the Southern Cross was clear and bright. The air was warm and soft as velvet.

Judy leaned on the railing of the wharf. Jon stood behind her with his hands on her shoulders. He ran the forefinger of one hand idly around the scoop neckline of her dress. Then he began to not quite caress the nape of her neck, holding the palm of his hand just above her skin. A delicious shiver passed through her. It seemed as if all her nerve endings stood straight up, yearning toward his touch, and all of her yearned with them.

Someone on shore began playing a radio or a CD. The big band music of a former era throbbed out over the moonlit water.

Jon stood before her. His teeth and his white shirt gleamed in the dusky night. "This dance, milady?" he asked as he gave a little bow.

She moved into his arms. The soft curves of her slight body fit the hard planes of his perfectly. She was glad she'd worn flat shoes. High heels would not have done at all for dancing on the wharf. Her left hand rested lightly on his shoulder, and her right was clasped in his left. She danced on tiptoe. He bent his head to rest his cheek against her hair.

The music changed, and a vocalist sang an old love song. Jon drew back so as to look into Judy's eyes and sang with the vocalist. Judy joined in. They sang and danced, her head tilted up to his, her eyes captured by his gaze. The song ended, the saxophone once more became dominant, and they moved to the hypnotic rhythm of a waltz.

He drew her a little closer and brought their clasped hands up to rest on her shoulder, thumbs linked, her hand enveloped in his. Then their hands weren't clasped any more. Hers were locked behind his head. His arms held her in a tight embrace, and his lips nuzzled her neck and ear. They still moved to the pulsing music, the moon still rode in the northern sky, and the Southern Cross still beckoned.

Judy knew she was caught in a magic moment. Magic moments are often recognized only in retrospect, but she knew that whatever happened, whomever she married, this moment would remain always, a little jewel in her memory. She held her breath, fearful of breaking the enchantment, of bringing the magic moment to an end.

They stopped moving their feet, but the music still wove its spell, and their bodies still swayed to its rhythm. He moved his lips over her face, and then to her mouth.

"You're beautiful," he murmured, his hot breath brushing the side of her neck. "Your red hair, your freckles, your golden eyelashes. And your courage— your wonderful, wonderful courage, to come out here. By yourself. Why can't we be like this, together, for the rest of our lives?"

She froze in his arms. What did he mean? Had he just proposed to her? Had he even realized what he'd said?

She should get away. Right now. But she couldn't. She still clung to him, still tangled her hands in his hair, still welcomed his arms, tight around her, holding her close.

"You drive me crazy, Judy."

Her heart said *You drive me crazy, too,* but her lips were silent.

She forced herself to draw away, out of his arms. The magic moment had fled. They started up the hill.

"I'm going fishing tomorrow," he said. "You're welcome to come if you like, but I think you need some time and space to yourself right now. I'll leave the camper open for you in the morning. You'll have more room there to spread out, work on your writing, whatever you want. I'll be back about six." He added, "You might want to get tonight into your book before you forget any of it."

She was startled. He hadn't sounded sarcastic. "What do you mean?" she asked. "You wouldn't want me to use this for a book, would you?"

He shrugged lightly as he bent down and kissed her on the nose. "Why not? I would."

They reached her tent. He pulled her into his arms in one last embrace. "Good night, my love. My darling love—my sweetheart of the Bayside wharf."

She drew back and looked into his face, mesmerized. "Who are you, Jon Brown?" she said. "Who are you, and what do you want with me?"

Judy disappeared into her tent, and Jon stood alone. The magic moment was over for him, too, and he was uncomfortable. *So, Jon Brown,* he chided silently, *who is taking care of the caretaker?* What would he have done if she'd taken his words as a proposal and said yes? How would he have explained that one to her father?

"Well," he mused, talking aloud to himself, "maybe I'd have just married her. There'd be worse fates. If she'd have had me, that is." He smiled to himself. The possibility of any woman turning him down would be remote.

But she hadn't treated his words as a proposal of marriage. He'd escaped this time. He vowed to cut back on the sort of scene that would cause both of them to lose their heads the way they had tonight. Then too, it wasn't necessary. She wouldn't leave him now. He had her hooked.

The songs were safe. He'd keep on serenading her. No woman in her right mind would ever say, "Yes, I'll marry you" in response to the words of a song.

He had to sort out his feelings about himself, about this woman, about this bargain he had struck with Harold Gallant. Instead of entering the camper, he walked the road that led to the beach and sat in the shadows, watching the moon on the water and brooding.

Judy couldn't sleep. She tossed and turned and relived every kiss. Had he intended to propose? She'd known him less than a week. Marriages were forever, built on mutual trust and respect. They weren't built on a longing for a man you knew nothing about and who refused to give you any information.

She'd always visualized a long period of dating, visits with each other's friends and families, a formal engagement complete with a ring to dazzle jealous girlfriends, parties and showers, and then the long white dress and the walk up the aisle.

Moonlit dances on wharves with men she barely knew had never been part of her fantasy. Until she met Jon.

She couldn't stand it anymore. She got up and dressed in her swimsuit, a short white terry-cloth robe, and her beach sandals, prepared to walk along the beach where the water kissed the sand. She slipped quietly out of the tent. The stars were still bright. The moon, almost down, hung low in the west.

The beach was right over the hill. She hadn't been there yet, but the road sign was clear, and she knew it was only a short walk. She felt almost like a sneak thief as she quietly zipped the tent flap behind her and stole out of the campground. The town slept. No dog barked nor bird sang. She walked stealthily up the street marked Beach Road, and, sure enough, she was soon there. The beach was a long, lovely curve of white sand. The last glimmer of the moon reflected on the water. It was a warm and windless night, and only gentle waves lapped the shore.

She put one toe, still with her sandals on, gingerly into the water. The ocean was warm, an extension of the balmy night. No one was around. The few beach homes were in darkness and at some distance from her. Subconsciously she must have intended to swim all along, or she wouldn't have dressed for it.

She knew that swimming alone was dangerous, but she'd stay close to shore and be careful. There was very little wave motion. She'd do it. She would. Before she lost her nerve, she would. She slipped off her robe and sandals, piling them carefully on the beach. Then she slid smoothly into the water.

The silky water enveloped and relaxed her, and she swam in it joyfully, cleansing herself of the troubling thoughts of the long night. She swam and floated and plunged and dived, dropping worries with every stroke.

The moon dipped below the horizon. The sky lightened and the stars began to fade. Reluctantly Judy swam to shore and ran to her robe. She didn't have a towel, but that didn't matter. The air was so warm that even five minutes would partially dry her. There wasn't anyone around, and it was still quite dark. She spread the robe and lay down on her stomach. *Just five minutes,* she told herself.

When she awoke, the sun shone on her. Anyone seeing her would think she was some crazy woman sleeping overnight on the beach. Panic-stricken, she

looked around, but she appeared to be totally alone.
She slipped into her robe and sandals, scuttled up the
road, sneaked into the campground, and dived for the
comfort of her tent. It was only 7:00. She got back
into her pajamas, and lay on top of the sleeping bag
because the morning sun had already warmed up the
tent. Within minutes she was asleep again.

When Judy awoke, it was almost noon, and the tent
was unbearably hot. She was sticky with sweat. Dried
salt crystals clung to her skin and hair. The clean, cool
feeling of the morning had fled. Jon had offered her
the camper, and she told herself she had an obligation
to use it. After all, he'd left it unlocked.

After a shower and a dreary breakfast in the camp
kitchen, deserted at this hour, Judy took her notebook
and went to the camper. Compared to the tent, it was
delightful. The screened windows were open to take
advantage of every scrap of breeze, and, before he left,
Jon had carefully closed the drapes on every window
that might catch the morning sun. Everything was
neat. Even though Jon had left early, there were no
dirty dishes in the sink. Judy thought guiltily of her
own sleeping bag and clothes thrown untidily on the
tent floor.

There was a briefcase beside the table. Ah, briefcase. That probably eliminated football player as Jon's
profession. It crossed Judy's mind that some of the
information she sought might well be in that briefcase,
but her moral code didn't permit snooping.

Perhaps she should cook dinner for him. He'd

cooked for her, made lunch for her, taken her out last night. Her contributions had been limited to eating. Quickly she planned her menu—it had to be good, but simple enough that she couldn't mess up.

She'd never done much cooking. Her mother hadn't worked outside the home, and it had been easy for Judy to do her homework or read a book while her mother made meals. After she'd begun teaching and got her own apartment, she'd been so busy with lesson plans and correcting that she'd relied on convenience food.

She smiled to herself as she chose a meal that seemed foolproof. Steak—broiled unless he wished to barbecue—new potatoes, mushrooms, green salad. And, a little more risky, if she could find someone downtown to tell her how to make a Pavlova—that New Zealand delicacy of meringue and whipped cream and fresh fruit—she'd do it. Otherwise, strawberries and rich New Zealand cream should do just fine.

She made her shopping list and set off downtown.

Yes, the nice woman at the grocery store could tell her exactly how to make Pavlova. There was really nothing to it. Judy wrote down the recipe, then added eggs, castor sugar, and cornstarch to her grocery list and bought her groceries, except for the steak.

She walked back to the butcher shop. It was a real old-fashioned butcher shop, handling nothing but meat. She asked the butcher for a couple of nice filets for barbecuing. He cut them in front of her, and wrapped them in waxed paper and then in newspaper.

There wasn't much to prepare except the Pavlova, so she started on the meringue. If that failed, there'd still be the strawberries and cream. But it didn't fail. It came out light and fluffy and beautifully done. She set it aside, then washed the potatoes and put them into a pot ready to cook, washed the mushrooms and put them into a pan, made the salad and put it into the fridge. Except for whipping the cream, she was ready with three hours to spare.

She took out her notebook and settled herself at the table, but she couldn't write. She regretted the computer she'd left sitting on her desk back in Maine. Computer or notebook, she had to get going on the book if she intended to finish it before the next school year started.

It wasn't any use. She couldn't do anything until she had this dashing and disturbing man out of her system. All she could do was think about the scene on the Bayside wharf and what Jon's intentions were.

In desperation, she went back to her tent, got a paperback novel, and brought it to the camper. She curled up to read until Jon got home—*No*, she corrected herself, *not home, but back.* "Home" sounded like a married woman waiting for her husband.

He came in shortly before six. "Hi. Glad to see you here. I did fleetingly wonder what I'd do if you'd taken off again." Then he saw the meringue and pots and pans. "Hmm. Good for you. What's for supper?"

"Steak," she said. "I'll broil it now unless you'd rather barbecue. Any luck?"

"Yep. Threw them back after the guide took my

picture." He put his camera on the counter. "Yes, I'd like to barbecue. There are gas barbecues here in the campground. I'll have a shower and then cook."

She started the potatoes and mushrooms and began to whip the cream. Jon came out of the shower, freshly shaved, hair wet, and wearing clean cutoffs, still tucking in his shirt. It was all very domestic. He took the meat and disappeared. She put the finishing touches to the meal, and when he came back everything was ready.

The dinner was good, and she glowed with pleasure when he told her so. When they had finished, he made tea while she cleared the table. It was all so comfortable she could hardly believe this was the same man she'd danced with last night.

But she couldn't just let things pass. She'd thought about him and thought about him, and wondered what to do. She'd start with another attempt to find out who he was, and then she'd try to gain some perspective about him.

They were seated at the clean table with cups of tea.

"Jon," she said, looking diligently at her fingernails, "you've got me so crazy I don't know whether I'm coming or going. There's no point in pretending otherwise, because you know. I can't write. I can't sleep." She took another deep breath. "The worst of it is, I don't even know who you are."

He smiled his irresistible smile. "I've told you that. I'm plain Jon Brown from Boston."

"Yeah, right. Married? Single?"

"I told you that."

"And, of course, what you told me was the truth. You might be a professional burglar for all I know, but I'm supposed to believe that every word coming out of your mouth is absolute truth. What do you work at?"

"I'm not quite ready to tell you that."

"Why not? Maybe you really are a burglar? Or a drug smuggler? Or a money launderer?"

"All I can do is repeat what I told you before. If you're uncomfortable about me, we'll go to the police station and have them vouch for me."

"But why? If there's nothing to hide, why don't you just tell me? And why are you following me around?"

"I promised—" He stopped abruptly as if he realized what he'd nearly said.

"You promised whom what?" she challenged as she jerked her head up and finally looked at him.

"Myself," he said. "I promised myself that I'd take good care of you."

"What? What do you mean, take care of me? I'm not a child. I don't need to be taken care of. I can take care of myself."

"Of course you can," he said. "Just like you picked up your car and drove it. Just like you handled yourself so well on the road to Bayside. Anyway, Judy, just let's say you've aroused my better instincts. Don't begrudge a man his better instincts."

She glared at him.

"Better instincts. Huh. That doesn't have much to do with telling me what you do for a living. I'll show you whether I can take care of myself. I'll leave tomorrow," she said. "I'll get out of your way. You won't have to bother with me anymore."

"No!" There was something almost desperate about the way he roared the word.

She flinched as if he had struck her, and he said, more quietly, "No, Judy. Please don't leave. I apologize for the things I said. I know you can take care of yourself. You wouldn't be here otherwise. I can't lose you. Please?

He ran the fingers of one hand through his curls, obviously stalling. "Look, I think I've made you uncomfortable. Why don't we just have fun together, be good friends. I'll give you a chance to get to know me as something more than a sensational kisser. Okay?"

She scowled, then nodded. After all, she couldn't picture life here without Jon Brown.

He got up, pulled her to her feet, and gave her a brief hug and a gentle kiss.

"I'll take care of the dishes, Judy."

He touched her forehead with his. "I can still keep serenading you? You can't ask me to give up everything, can you, and that's fun."

She released her held breath and gave him a gamin grim. "Yes," she said, "it is fun, isn't it?" and she scampered off into the night.

She was nearly asleep when she heard the strumming of the guitar and the sequence of chords that meant her song would follow. She was beginning to enjoy the ritual.

"I wooed you in Auckland; I'll wed you in Christchurch

I'll chase you all over from the east to the west.
Your cheeks are like roses, your lips like ripe
  cherries
But when you swim in the moonlight, I love you the
  best."

She sat bolt upright in her sleeping bag. The nerve of him. She tumbled out of bed and grabbed the first thing she could find, one of her sneakers.

"You rat!" she screamed, as she unzipped the tent and fired it at him.

She zipped the tent and crawled back into the bag. A moment later, a hand holding a shoe appeared under the zipper.

"You lost something, darlin'. By the way, camp rules call for silence after ten-thirty. No screaming."

She heard him chuckle as he walked away.

If she'd intended to find out about him and keep distance between them, her day's efforts had been a distinct bust.

Chapter Five

The days of Judy's New Zealand idyll fell into an easy pattern. She regained strength and energy with every passing day. She and Jon had drifted into sharing meals. Sometimes Judy cooked, sometimes Jon did, sometimes they both did. He accepted her insistence on paying for half the groceries with a sort of amused tolerance. Judy became more comfortable, and finally really and truly accepted that he meant her no harm. They drifted into the cheerful, open friendship he had promised her.

They explored hiking trails and frequently tramped the hills and valleys for a half day or for a full day, carrying sandwiches and water for their noon meal. She knew that Jon's insistence on frequent rest stops was out of consideration for her. Although her health was almost back to normal, she appreciated his concern. Occasionally they hired horses instead of walking. Other times they swam and lay on golden beaches under the gentle New Zealand skies.

Evening sing-alongs became more frequent. The first time, Judy was already in bed when the singing began. When she heard the first notes, she scrambled into jeans and a sweater. She wouldn't give Jon another chance to accuse her of being shy—even if it was true. He met her, threw one arm around her shoulders, and escorted her to the circle of people on the hillside.

He gave her a little squeeze as he said, "This is Judy, my best friend."

There was a chorus of greetings. Jon sat on the grass and pulled her down beside him. The young blond woman who was seated on the other side of Jon sat in sullen silence as the singing resumed. Judy joined in happily and, although she knew it was petty of her, felt smugly satisfied that Jon preferred her to the exquisite creature seated on his other side.

During this time, although Jon still caressed and stroked her hair, he had, as he'd promised, backed off on the embraces that confused her. She missed the kisses but was sensible enough to feel relieved.

Life had become a lovely dream. The only bad times came when she wrote to her parents. She simply couldn't tell them the truth, fearing they'd misunderstand and be hurt. Yet Jon had become so much a part of her life that it was increasingly difficult to avoid mentioning him.

When they traveled, he took the lead, and she followed. She and her vehicle were on much better terms, to the point that she was beginning to view the red car with something like affection. She handled driving on

the left-hand side of the road with increasing confidence as they crossed the country and worked their
way slowly down the western coast.

They drove back through Auckland in the early
morning when the streets were empty. Once they had
settled into a campground, he left her in the camper
and used her car to drive back to the city for meetings.

He was gone three full days, and, when he returned,
the mail which he brought her included the letter from
Walter, the letter she'd tried to forget, the letter she'd
begun to hope would never come. But it had come,
and she had to deal with it. Walter had taken vacation
time the second and third weeks of March, and he was
coming to New Zealand. She said nothing to Jon, but
wrote to Walter, telling him that when his plans were
finalized he was to write to her and send the letter to
Rotorua, general delivery.

Jon's absences soon became a pattern. He usually
disappeared at least once a week, sometimes for just
a day, sometimes for up to three days. She was curious
and she missed him, but she no longer saw the meetings as ominous. She still played her private guessing
games about his profession but had pretty well decided
he was in business. With his looks and his voice, he
could have been an entertainer, but then he would have
been absent on weekends.

She found that she was making progress on her
writing. Once she let the hero have dark curls and
piercing blue eyes, the story took care of itself. Jon
had actually encouraged her to use bits and pieces
from their relationship. He'd said the book would

sound more realistic if she wrote about things she'd experienced, and he'd insisted that she take detailed notes on the places they visited so her descriptions would be authentic. It almost seemed as if he knew about writing, but he seemed to know about everything else, so why not?

After they left the Auckland area they went back to the east coast. One day when she was trailing him on the highway, she saw a real Gypsy caravan. Jon had passed it, and she followed it for some time. The homemade camper of plywood painted brown was set on an old truck. At the back was a small porch, complete with carved railings and a covered roof. Two small children sat on the porch. Behind them were three stained-glass windows. It was a delightful picture, and she wished she could share her pleasure with Jon.

After dinner, they crossed the road that lay between their campground and the beach, another long and lovely beach. They walked and then sat on the hard-packed sand. She sat between Jon's knees, leaning against him. His arms were draped loosely around her shoulders. He caressed her jaw casually with his thumb and nuzzled her hair, occasionally dropping a light kiss on her head or the back of her neck. She was very content. *This must be what a good marriage is like,* she thought dreamily.

In the comfortable atmosphere between them, she told him about the Gypsy caravan.

"It was just like the stories and poems we had in

school when I was a little kid. I wanted to share it with you, not later, but at the time."

"I know," he said. "I saw it and felt the same." He went on, "This might be a good time to bring up something I've been thinking about for a while."

"Hmm?"

"Well, this isn't the only thing. Sometimes I pass a hiking trail, and I think, 'I wonder if Judy'd like to do that,' but it's awkward to stop the whole procession. And I know you're on a tight budget."

"Okay, Jon, get to the point." The mention of money annoyed her. Was he about to offer to pay some of her expenses? She'd just become drowsy and contented and now had the uncomfortable feeling she was going to be stirred up.

"All right. The point is this. Why don't you, next time there's a chance, turn Betsy or Lulubelle or whatever you call her back to the rental company, and we'll both travel in the camper."

She sat bolt upright. "No!" she burst out. "I can't do that. It wouldn't be right."

"No, Judy," he said patiently, "you'd keep the tent. We'd just drive together. We're already eating meals together. I can't see that this would compromise you any more. If your pride needs a sop, you can apply part of your savings to the camper rental."

He continued idly caressing her jaw with his thumb. He was talking casually, not sounding at all like a person who'd just dropped a bombshell.

She shook her head vigorously and repeated stubbornly, "No, I can't. I just can't. It wouldn't be right."

She added caustically, "And I'm sure when I told my parents and then reassured them with, 'But I always pitch my little tent at night,' they'd be really impressed. My dad would come right out and drag me home. Whether I'm a liberated woman or not."

"Don't be too sure of that," he said softly. "So how about it?"

"Look," she said, "I know I don't have to obey my parents anymore. It's just that that's not the way they brought me up and they'd be very very hurt. I'm sorry. I'll still feel that way when I'm fifty."

"Yes. I respect that. But I'm not suggesting anything more than just saving a bit of money and making things more convenient."

She set her teeth and shook her head. Never mind her parents. The nerve of Jon Brown. As if he should make all the decisions. Who drove what? Who did what? Who ate and slept where?

"You won't even tell me who you are, and here you're suggesting I return the car so I'll be totally dependent on you. Forget it, mystery man. You talk like a college professor when you forget you're masquerading as a hick. Who are you anyway?"

He seemed undisturbed by the outburst. "You'll find out all in good time, my lovely."

He looked down at her. "So what about turning in the car?" he said again.

"No," she said. "No. N-O. Friendship is a two-way street. You expect me to trust you without reservation. How about you trusting me enough to confide in me? Get the message?"

"Okay." He raised his hands in a gesture of capitulation. We keep the camper, Lulubelle, and the tent. Now just lean back and relax again."

She shouldn't, but she did. She settled back comfortably against him. "I couldn't sleep after that night on the wharf, you know."

His arms tightened around her. "I know, Judy. I couldn't either. That was one of the most beautiful moments of my life—you, your white dress in the moonlight, the music." His voice became low, mesmerizing her as he murmured, "My sweetheart of the Bayside wharf."

"How long were you there? On the beach, I mean?"

"Longer than you were. I came down to be alone with my thoughts." He chuckled. "The main difference was that I was fully dressed. I heard you coming and withdrew into the shadows. Then when I realized what you were up to I didn't want to startle you, and I told myself I had to stay to protect you in case you got into trouble in the water or in case someone came along whose intentions weren't quite as honorable as mine."

His voice was husky. "You were so beautiful, just like the dolphins, so beautiful I could have cried. And then after you left, I went back to the campground and down to the wharf for the fishing boat."

A lump formed in her throat, and she sat quietly for a moment. Then she stirred and mused, "What will the future be like, Jon?" She watched the Southern Cross for a moment of silence before she said, "What's in the stars for us?"

He paused, as if trying to choose his words carefully, but when he continued there was a reckless note in his voice.

"Oh," he said, "there'll be a lot of times like this—just the two of us, talking and being close. And there'll be lots of times like that night on the Bayside wharf. I've backed off on that because we don't seem to handle it very well, but if we were married, it wouldn't end with my sending you back to a tent."

"I didn't mean *that*," she protested. "I meant us, separately, you and me—as individuals." She meditated a few moments longer. "I wonder whom we will marry, Jon, you and I? What will you want of your wife? In real life. Will you expect her to sharpen skates, or milk cows?"

He laughed. "Only if she wants to, darlin'. If her heart is really set on milking cows, I suppose we could buy a hobby farm close enough to a train station that I could commute to work. Otherwise, I have a condo in downtown Boston that I sort of assumed I'd use to start married life."

It was hard for her to imagine—her romantic rover shedding the old hat and the faded cutoffs for a tie and a dark suit and riding the commuter train to work. Not, mind you, that she didn't suspect that right now he went through this metamorphosis, as soon as he was out of her sight, every time he went to one of his meetings. But she seemed to be on the trail of more information than she'd ever had before, so she didn't want to disrupt it.

"Tell me about it," she prompted.

"Well, it's really very comfortable. It has two bedrooms and a study. If you were my wife and wanted to write, I'd make the smaller bedroom into a study for you, and you could write your books while I was at work.

"And after the kids came, we could buy a house, and you could walk them in the park in their little strollers and when they were older we'd go together to parent–teacher nights to discuss their spelling."

His lips nuzzled her ear, and his voice was so low and hypnotic that when he said, "You do want kids?" she just answered, "Oh, yes." She remembered she was angry about his insisting on behaving as if she were going to be his wife and added hastily, "Speaking in general terms, of course."

"Of course," he murmured. "And by time we have kids you'll know whether your books are selling, and if they are we'll hire a nanny so you'll have time to keep up your writing."

It all seemed like a beautiful dream, such a lovely lifestyle, but was any of it true?

And, to Jon Brown, as he talked, it seemed a lovely lifestyle too. He remembered the Bayside beach, and saw her again, white in the moonlight. Yes, there could be worse fates than coming home every night to this delicious redhead.

What was standing in the way? Her father? Yes, her father had asked him to take care of her, not to fall in love with her. Were these feelings love? The enchantment with the emerald eyes and the golden eyelashes?

The desperate need to keep her from harm, and not only because of the promise to her parents? The contentment he'd felt when he'd barbecued while she put the finishing touches on their meal, just as if she were his wife?

They enjoyed the same things—beaches, hikes, horseback rides.

He knew about love, for heaven's sake. He was a literature professor. In his spare time, he wrote novels. But was this really what love was—this combination of longing and content?

Never mind. He'd better forget about it for now. After this trip was over, he'd be free of the obligations to her father and could pursue her as he wished.

He looked down at Judy. "Shouldn't you retire?" he said.

When she had gone, he sang softly and thought of her.

The next day, as Judy followed Jon on the highway, they passed a herd of sheep. They were driving on a hilly winding road, past wide streambeds full of sand and gravel, so full of gravel that trucks were hauling it to use on the roads. Small shallow rivers meandered through these wide gravel beds, but Judy suspected that during a rain, water rushing down from the hills would fill the banks to overflowing.

Suddenly, on a sharp corner, Jon flicked his brake lights and stopped by the side of the road. Judy pulled up behind him. He came back to the car, sliding into the passenger seat, leaving the door open because of the heat.

"We'll just sit here for a while," he said. "There's a shepherd moving sheep up ahead. We could drive through slowly, but we're in no rush, so I thought this time we'll watch something together. We'll wait for them to go by before we move on. The vanguard should be almost here."

Sure enough, the front group of sheep, newly shorn, came along the road, walking daintily on sharp pointed hooves. With them walked a herdsman and two watchful dogs that looked like shorthaired black-and-white collies.

Then came the mass of sheep, walking up the highway as if they owned it, any straggler soon being put in place by the swift and silent dogs. There seemed to be a sea of sheep, and then, at last, the mass thinned and passed. Two more dogs and a man on horseback brought up the rear.

"The dogs seem to be doing all the work," Judy said.

"Yes, they respond perfectly to either whistles or spoken commands."

They sat in silence for a moment after the sheep had gone. Then Jon said, "We're stopped anyway. Let's have tea."

They'd picked up the New Zealand custom of stopping for tea in the middle of the morning and afternoon, and now they walked up to the camper. Jon made tea, strong and hot, while Judy put out mugs and cookies. Jon pored over the map.

"I'm committed to Gisborne on Wednesday," he said. "That gives us the rest of today and tomorrow to get there. No problem. We can take our time."

Judy cleared her throat. She'd written to Walter a month ago, at the end of January. "I'd really like to get to Rotorua by Friday," she said. "That's my next point on my itinerary where I pick up mail."

Jon looked surprised. They'd both come to take for granted that Jon would choose the route to correspond with his meetings. By some fortunate coincidence, the itinerary Judy had worked out with her parents seemed very close to his. She wondered how Jon would react to her request, because she'd never shown any concern about mail pickups before. However, he didn't say anything, but just checked the map.

"That shouldn't be a problem," he said. "I can get away from Gisborne about three on Wednesday. If we follow the highway for the first leg rather than trying to cut through the hills, by night we should reach a nice campground I know about that's on a lake. If we don't make Rotorua by time the post office closes on Thursday, we'll be there Friday morning for sure."

She was relieved. "Good. That'll be fine."

Jon kept his word. On Wednesday, they headed out of Gisborne a few minutes after three.

They made good time on the first stretch of road. Judy followed easily, her mind busy with things other than the condition of the road.

She felt disturbed and guilty about her reasons for having to pick up mail that week, but if Walter was coming the second week in March, she really had to know the details. She hadn't told Jon anything about Walter. At the Bangor airport, she'd referred to him as a friend, but had never mentioned Walter's vague hopes of coming out for his vacation.

She had, in the moments she remembered Walter existed, hoped he wouldn't come, but she really had no reason to tell him not to. She could hardly tell him he couldn't come because she spent all her time with the total stranger he'd referred to as the "beach bum" in Bangor. Without telling him about Jon, she'd had no reason to discourage him from coming.

However, the letter Jon had picked up in Auckland had dashed any wish that the vague hopes would never materialize. They'd become real plans with real dates, and it had been too late then to tell him not to come. She couldn't delay the letter she'd sent, but she'd delayed telling Jon.

She knew that when she picked up the next letter she'd have to explain. At that point, there'd be only a week until Walter arrived. She supposed he'd fly into Auckland. It wouldn't take long to go back. Hopefully, Jon would have meetings to amuse him somewhere next week, and she could meet Walter on her own.

At the end of the main highway, they ate a hurried meal and then swung inland. At first, the road was a lovely change. It was paved, and wound and dipped through stands of shady trees. The native ferns and pongas had been left behind, and the tall trees that lined the road were the so-called exotic trees—pines and poplars and willows.

Suddenly the road narrowed. The sky darkened and a gusting wind kicked up dust and blew branches off trees. Judy tried not to think about the possibility of one of these falling on the roof of her car. She passed construction zones and hydroelectric projects. With every passing mile, the road became higher and hillier.

She knew if she dropped back further behind Jon, there'd be less dust, but he seemed her only security on this hostile road, and she couldn't bear to increase the distance between them. The gusts of wind began driving sporadic sheets of rain before them, turning some of the dust clouds all around her to smears of mud on the windshield.

Eventually they reached the lake, and she looked forward to stopping, but the narrow road still wound on and on with no campground in sight. When they eventually did reach the campground, Jon checked in at the office and then drove the camper to his site. The campground itself in better weather would have been delightful. It was on the lake, and wild ducks shared the grounds with the tourists. Judy drove her car up beside Jon's camper and darted through the rain to its shelter.

They made and ate bacon-and-egg sandwiches.

Jon looked at her with concern. "Let me take the tent tonight," he said. "It's not a fit night for you to sleep out there."

She shook her head stubbornly. "I can't. It wouldn't be right."

"All right," he said, "but if you and that tent both blow into the lake, remember I told you so. And I couldn't get two sites together, so it won't be easy for you to just duck back in." He went on, "It's pretty windy, so I'd better help you with the tent."

He put on a yellow slicker. She turned up the collar of her jacket. They walked through the rain, Jon carrying the tent. Wolf whistles came through the open door of a big camper.

"Hey, cowboy," came a voice, "how about sharing. You don't need her all to yourself."

Judy shrank closer to Jon, and he put his arm around her. "Just a couple of drunk fishermen, darlin'. I suspect they're all bluff, but I really wish you'd take the camper. It has a good lock."

She shook her head again, adamant.

When the tent was finally up, Judy went back for her sleeping bag and tote bag while Jon double-checked the pegs. Again she heard whistles and comments, louder and ruder than the first ones had been. She was frightened, but she wasn't going to put Jon out in the rain while she used his camper. When she came back with her things, Jon was at the big camper, talking to the fishermen. They suddenly seemed very quiet.

Jon helped her spread out her sleeping bag before they went back to the camper for the evening. They usually had tea and played cribbage or read. Sometimes she asked his advice on passages of her writing.

"What did you say to them?" she asked when they were back in the camper.

"Nothing much. I just suggested that unless they

wanted their next of kin to drag the lake for their bodies, they'd better shut up and leave you alone."

"Oh," was all she could think of to say.

Later Jon walked her to her tent. The fishermen had closed up their camper. Judy got into her sleeping bag. The rain pounded against the canvas, and the howling wind seemed determined to blow the tent completely off its moorings. She was cold and uneasy and couldn't sleep. There was increasing noise around her, and she imagined it to be the drunks full of newfound courage now that Jon had gone.

Finally, she screwed up every ounce of courage she had and peered out. She nearly screamed aloud. A dark shape lay on the ground before her tent. The scream died in her throat when she saw the dear familiar Aussie hat, and she realized that Jon was sleeping in the rain, across the doorway of her tent.

Quietly she crawled back into her sleeping bag, recognizing that tonight marked another subtle advance in their relationship. She slept soundly and when she awoke, the sun was beating on her tent, the wind had died, and Jon was gone.

On Friday morning, when they reached Rotorua, Judy went to the post office while Jon left to buy groceries. The letter from Walter was there. Judy sat at a table in the post office lobby and opened it.

Walter wasn't coming to Auckland as she'd assumed. He was coming to Queenstown, first to Christchurch, and then on a local flight to Queenstown a week from Monday. He had so little time, he said, that it seemed sensible to stay in one location, and the Queenstown–Milford Sound area seemed to have a lot to offer.

Judy was aghast. Queenstown was almost at the south end of the South Island, and here she was up in the middle of the North Island. True, she still had over a week, depending on what kind of luck she had with ferry reservations.

She could hardly expect Jon to bail her out of this one. She'd be lucky if he didn't drive off into the sunset and never look back when he heard about it, never mind taking responsibility for getting her there.

There was no point phoning Walter. Arrangements like that couldn't be changed, and when he had come all that way, to refuse to see him would be unthinkable. No, she had to go through with it, no matter what.

She read on. He'd made reservations for both of them. She felt more than a twinge of guilt when she read the name of the expensive hotel. Well, regardless of Walter's intentions, budget or no budget, she'd pay her own hotel bill when she checked in.

They would use her car, Walter wrote, and that would be her contribution to the vacation. Then near the end of his vacation they would do the Milford Track walk. He knew she'd wanted to do this, so he'd made reservations for them.

Judy was thoughtful. Walter seemed to assume she would spend the whole two weeks with him. And why shouldn't he? The few postcards she'd sent him suggested she was having a wonderful time—all by herself. He saw her parents frequently, and the letters she'd sent to them suggested she was having a wonderful time—all by herself.

She was troubled as she put her mail into her purse and went back to the parked vehicles. Jon was in the camper, loading groceries into the fridge. When he asked her if she'd got the mail she was expecting, she nodded.

She had to tell him, but she couldn't. They checked into a campground, and she didn't say anything. They made and ate dinner, and she didn't say anything. They pored over brochures of what to do the next day, and she didn't say anything.

The next day they drove out of town for a sheep-shearing demonstration. Judy wasn't sure what to expect, but she was quite sure it would entail sitting on the old corral surrounded by dust and smells and flies.

She certainly was not prepared for what she found— an indoor auditorium, spotlessly clean and odorless, with a stage at the front and plug-ins by every seat for instantaneous translation into other languages. On stage was a double row of platforms arranged like stair steps, each platform labeled with the name of a breed of sheep. At the side of the auditorium were small pens with the sheep.

The show started. Each sheep, when released, rushed to its own platform, motivated by a little can of food. The narrator told a bit about each breed, and then gave a dazzling demonstration of shearing. Judy was so engrossed that she almost forgot her problem. After the shearing, three black-and-tan barking sheep dogs put on their show, and, later, outside, lovely swift and silent sheep dogs herded on command.

When the show was over, Jon and Judy went into the gift shop. The problems flooded back. Judy nibbled at the side of her thumb. She saw Jon look at her oddly, but she couldn't tell him in the middle of a gift shop, for Pete's sake.

They ate lunch in the café next to the arena, but that didn't seem to be a good place either. After lunch, they went to see some hot springs. Somehow all this hot, plopping gray mud didn't supply the right atmosphere. Judy's mind wasn't on the mud—her mind was on her problem. She kept chewing nervously at the side of her thumb.

Jon's time for serious conversations seemed to be after the evening meal when they were having tea. Judy nibbled her thumb and tried to get up her nerve.

Jon spoke as he sat across from her, leaning forward, cradling his cup. "Okay, Judy, what's bothering you? Out with it, darlin'."

She gave him a hunted, desperate look.

"There's no point holding it back. Was there something in the mail that upset you? Something wrong at home?"

"No, no-nothing's wrong at home. I-I-you—oh, I should have said something long ago." It came in a rush then. "Walter—that's the friend who dropped me at the airport—wanted to come out for his vacation. We—I—that is, I didn't know you then, and I told him he could—as long as he understood we were just friends—and I haven't told anybody about you—I mean, how could I?"

Jon sat in silence.

She knew it. She'd blown it. Jon would leave her now. And yes, she cared.

The silence became oppressive. Finally Jon stirred. "Look," he said, "I've got to be by myself for a while to deal with this." There was a pause as he looked at her. She knew her panic showed in her face. He continued. "It'll be okay. It's just that I need a little space right now. I'm going for a walk. Give me half an hour. Then we'll talk about what to do."

He kissed the top of her head and eased out the door.

Chapter Six

Outside, Jon drew a deep breath of evening air. It was dark, but the night was clear. He leaned on the back of Judy's car, hands in pockets and stared at the Southern Cross.

He was falling in love with her, he knew. He'd been falling in love with her ever since the night in Bayside. The long cozy chats on beaches and the quiet nights in the camper when they read or played cards had only drawn him in deeper.

He left the car and walked in long strides down to the beach, where he sat and gazed at the water.

Certainly, he was ready for marriage. For three or four years now, he'd become increasingly discontented with pointless dates and endless parties. He wanted his own home, a woman he loved to share it, children. A number of things had held him back.

The first was his parents' marriage. His father had gone to England on a student exchange program back in the early fifties. He'd married a pretty Scottish girl overseas a week after they met, and they still behaved as though they were on their honeymoon.

It had been embarrassing when he was a teenager. Even though they'd thought their family complete, the standard boy and girl, Jon had turned up when his parents were in their forties. That meant when he was a teenager, by teenager standards they were really old. It had been mortifying. He'd bring friends home and they'd find his parents necking in the kitchen or cuddled up in front of the TV. When they went for walks they held hands, and when his dad came home from work, his mother acted as if he'd just returned from a peacekeeping mission on Mars.

He hadn't stayed a teenager forever. As he grew into adulthood and looked at the world around him, he'd realized what a rare and precious love he'd been privileged to grow up with, and had vowed he wouldn't settle for anything less.

Then, in recent years, he'd watched the relationships of his friends and acquaintances—the divorces, the affairs, the marriages that limped along in the midst of indifference or downright hostility. He'd often wondered if the marriage he wanted still existed. He certainly wasn't going to find it with the brittle beauties he dated because his agent thought the publicity would be good for book sales.

Then Judy had come into his life.

The memory of that night on the wharf in Bayside and of seeing her swimming in the moonlight at the beach haunted him constantly.

He could have the marriage he wanted with Judy.

With Judy, there would be no affairs, no coexistence of hostile strangers. When they weren't driving each other crazy, they had a comfortable relationship.

So what was the problem?

The first problem was that he'd intended to take more time. He'd anticipated that this lovely idyll would drift along for another three months or so before he had to make a decision.

The second was her parents. Harold Gallant, to whom he owed a great deal, had, if he was going to be honest about it, asked him to be a baby-sitter to Judy. He'd also hinted that a baby-sitter was all he was to be. There seemed to be a serious conflict of interest here, and he wasn't sure how to handle it. He'd try to work through Marian. Marian, he was sure, would be on his side if she thought that he really loved Judy and was serious about her.

He wasn't sure why Harold had been so adamant, but he suspected it had to do with Jon's public image, that Harold didn't want his daughter drawn into a synthetic way of life. If that were the reason, he'd try to reassure him that Jonathan Marlowe, sophisticate and jet-setter, existed only in the imaginations of the media.

However, this changed things. He had to make up his mind, right now, one way or the other. He wasn't sure what Judy's relationship with Walter was, but he knew it wouldn't be fair to work on winning her away from Walter unless he was sure he himself intended to play for keeps.

Otherwise, he'd make very sure that afterward,

they'd be friends only. Even the songs would have to disappear. She'd think that jealousy had driven him away. Eventually, New Zealand and her memories of him would take on a hazy romantic tinge, her bit of nostalgia to treasure always.

But if he decided he still wanted her— He dreamed of having her at home, of protecting her always, but that would be up to her. He was no male chauvinist pig. If she needed to teach, or to write, to feel complete, he would support her in her choice, and he would be sure that she didn't wear herself out doing two full-time jobs, as so many working wives and mothers did.

He skipped a rock across the water, and got to his feet. How could he ever have felt there was a decision to make? He would have to let her go now, but after her two weeks with Walter was up, he'd pursue her in earnest. He'd woo her all over New Zealand and wed her in Christchurch, just as in the words of the song.

In the meantime, he'd continue to be plain Jon Brown to keep the mystery in the romance. He couldn't take a chance on her finding out too soon and linking him with her father. That was the one thing that might make her refuse him, that might wound her pride so much she would leave him.

As soon as she got back from her tour guide duties, he'd propose seriously and not let up until she said yes. Then he'd have her come to his first lecture in Christchurch, and she would discover who he was.

Eventually, he supposed he'd have to tell her how

the whole thing started. He smiled to himself. Perhaps shortly after the birth of their third child would be about right. She should be able to handle it by then.

His half hour was up. He started back to the camper, ready to step once more into his role.

The arrogance of him, Judy thought. He'd just walked out, left her in turmoil for half an hour, and now that he'd returned, there he was, just sitting smiling, not a bit upset.

"All right. Walter is just a friend—from your point of view, anyway. He's coming for vacation and wants to see you. So what are you so upset about?"

She looked at him, speechless. "You've been following me around ever since the Bangor airport, serenading me and . . . and . . . and whatever, and you don't care if I spend two weeks with Walter?"

He bent forward across the table and reached for her hand, idly caressing the thumb she'd been chewing on all day. "Judy, does whether I care or not matter to you?"

She nodded.

He leaned back, still holding her hand. "Then I don't really see that I've anything to be concerned about. I'll miss you terribly for those couple of weeks, but other than that I can't see that it matters much one way or the other. Now, exactly where are you going and how soon do you have to be there?"

"A week from Monday, in Queenstown."

He whistled. "Queenstown? Now *that* matters. I wish you'd told me right away because of ferry bookings. I'll try first thing tomorrow. And I have meetings in Palmerston North on Tuesday and Wednesday. He stroked her hand. "Don't worry. I'll work it out."

She blinked and looked at him. It wasn't indifference—he was just so sure of himself that it really didn't matter. She reluctantly gathered up the remnants of her self-respect. "You don't have to come," she said. "I got myself into this on my own. It's up to me to handle it on my own."

"Yes," he said, "I do have to come. I'm not letting you drive that distance by yourself. But don't worry, I'll keep a low profile, and he'll never know I exist— at least not until our wedding picture appears in your local paper."

When she glared at him, he said, "Joke!"

He paused and looked impossibly serious. "Also, I'm afraid your perception of this may be very different from Walter's. Men usually don't spend a two-week vacation traveling halfway around the world just to see a friend. Not unless they're fantastically wealthy men, and if he were fantastically wealthy he wouldn't be limited to a two-week vacation. I'm afraid this whole thing may blow up in your face, and, if it does, I'm not leaving you to deal with things on your own. You see what I'm getting at?"

She nodded, but protested. "There won't be a problem. I made it very clear to him in the airport that if he came it would be just as a friend."

"Does he think of you as just a friend?" Jon asked abruptly.

"Well," she said, "I guess he hopes for more—but I told him."

He smiled the lazy smile that always made her heart beat faster and caused the pulse at the side of her neck to throb so that she was sure he could see it. "Some men don't take no for an answer very readily. Just in case you hadn't noticed.

"It's okay," he continued. "You've got to go through with it, the whole two weeks, if he really is satisfied with friendship. He's coming a long way and spending a lot of money. The least you can do is be a nice little tour guide. If he wants more than that, I'll make him sorry he ever heard of New Zealand. Otherwise, I deliver you. You show Walter a good time. You come back to me. Fair enough?"

"No. It's not. It seems like I don't have a thing to say about what I do. Do you think maybe you could just butt out and mind your own business? Besides, if you really feel the way about me you say you do, why aren't you jealous?"

"Jealous. Of Walter? Judy, you have to be kidding." He began to laugh, then stopped. "All right, you don't have to be so bristly about everything. I'm sure he's a very nice man, and he'll be a good provider for some nice dull woman. But not you, my lovely. Oh, no, not you. He'd not be man enough for you."

"And you would, I suppose, you arrogant—" She couldn't finish.

His white teeth gleamed in his tanned face as he appeared to be on the verge of breaking into laughter again, and his blue eyes seemed to burn right through her.

"Ah, yes, my lovely, I would, my sweetheart of the Bayside wharf. Remember? Maybe it's time for a little replay?"

"No." She snatched her hand away. "No, Jon. Please." She folded her hands into a little knot in front of her on the table and looked down at them.

"Ah, you didn't like it? Fooled me."

She shook her head stubbornly. "No, that's not the reason."

"Well then, darlin', what is the reason?"

"I liked it too much," she whispered. There, it was out, and she knew it wasn't any surprise to him.

"Ah, I could just say, 'I rest my case,' but suddenly I find the idea of a replay very appealing."

Her head told her to keep resisting. Her heart told her to fall into his arms.

"Come, my lovely. I won't hurt you, and if you attack me, I think I can beat you off."

He moved over on the sofa, to where there was no table, and held out his hand.

Her heart won. She stood up slowly and moved toward him almost as if she were being pulled on a string, as if she had no will of her own. Her outstretched hand touched his, and she was in his arms.

"Now," he said softly, "just in case you're starting to think of me as 'just a friend,' here's that replay I promised."

* * *

Judy came to the camper for breakfast. She'd been tempted to avoid him, but she wouldn't give him that satisfaction.

He knew though. She'd no doubt of that. He knew very well that she'd spent the night tossing restlessly, reliving every kiss. She sipped her black coffee and nibbled her toast.

"All right," he said. "You've got a two-week date with Walter. I'm sure he's a wonderful chap, and I'm not jealous, but I wanted to be very sure that you didn't forget me."

She had to smile in spite of herself. Forget him? He was arrogant and sure of himself, but he was so good to her and his kisses inflamed her and she was going to miss him so during those two weeks, and, yes, she loved him. She knew that now, but she wasn't about to admit it to him—not until he told her more.

"Look, Judy," he said. "You really do look awful. Flake out on the couch for an hour while I go downtown and see what I can do about the ferry. Okay?"

He kissed her lightly and went through the door whistling cheerfully. After she heard the car start up, she collapsed gratefully onto the sofa.

Jon was gone a couple of hours, and although he tried to come in quietly, she heard him and stirred. When he saw that she was awake, he set down the bag he was carrying and put on the kettle.

"Teatime, darlin'," he said cheerfully. "I got some hot bacon-and-egg pies at a bakery downtown. Breakfast seemed a bit of a write-off."

She stumbled to the bathroom and splashed cold

water over her face. The extra sleep had been a life-
saver. She felt a lot better, although it occurred to her
to wonder whether her physical stamina, improved
though she was, was yet up to doing the Milford
Track.

"Okay. Come sit down while I feed us."

She sat down across the table from him. He handed
her tea and slid a plate with one of the pies across the
table to her.

"We're in luck," he went on. "I got us on the ferry
for four o'clock on Thursday afternoon. That means I
can keep my appointments at Palmerston North, and
we'll still have three full days to get down the South
Island to Queenstown. We won't have a lot of time
for sight-seeing, but we won't have to drive danger-
ously either."

"But you really don't have to—" she protested, but
he cut her off.

"Oh, yes, I do. I'll be back to pick you up when the
two weeks are over."

"That won't be necessary," she said. "After all,
we're just friends."

"No. Just a friend is what Walter is. Remember?"

Judy loved Queenstown—the shops, the eating
places, the streets. Sunday evening she strolled with
Jon along the waterfront and around Queenstown Bay
to the park on the peninsula beyond. They walked beneath towering spruce trees, probably brought to this
place by homesick English emigrants a long, long time
ago, and they sauntered among flowerbeds and

through the rose garden. The summer evening crept slowly into dusk as they sat on a park bench and looked out over the water. Judy wore shorts and a shirt, with a long-sleeved pullover sweater for warmth against the evening air. Jon placed one arm loosely around her, and absentmindedly rubbed her shoulder. Neither of them spoke. Then he nuzzled her hair with his lips, and kissed her.

It was another replay of the Bayside wharf. Finally he whispered, his voice husky, "Enough. I couldn't let you go without reminding you whom you belonged to, and it seemed in bad taste to wait until tomorrow afternoon to do this."

His arms tightened around her as he murmured in her ear, "Judy, darlin', I'm going to miss you. We'll get married as soon as you've completed your time in the guided tour business. Okay?"

She stiffened in his arms. Married? He was more specific than he'd been on the wharf in Bayside. Married? It was tempting, very tempting, to have him forever, for her very own, this man with the looks of a movie star, and the physique of a quarterback.

But who was he? Was she prepared to marry a total stranger?

She wouldn't think about it now. She'd have lots of time for analyzing her feelings about Jon while she went through the motions of entertaining Walter.

They walked back to the campground, arms entwined.

In the morning, she wore her white dress again, this time with high-heeled shoes. It was the only time she'd dressed up in New Zealand except for that one mad night in Bayside. She watched Jon watch her.

She'd put her tent and sleeping bag into the camper, along with her extra luggage, keeping just the tote bag and one suitcase for the clothes she needed for the next two weeks. Jon had put the book she was working on in what he called his junk drawer, the kitchen drawer below the cutlery.

Now he watched her quietly as she made last-minute adjustments in her packing. His eyes were troubled.

"Sit down, Judy," he said finally, "and I'll make you a cup of tea before you go."

She'd just bet he would, and a half hour's worth of advice to go with it.

"I didn't tell you this before, because you were already feeling guilty about bothering me," he said when they were settled, "but I have to be in Wellington on Wednesday and Thursday this week."

"Oh," she said, embarrassed, "you mean you've got to turn around and drive back to Wellington, go across the ferry again?"

He shook his head. "No, I'll fly. I've already made the booking, and I'm delaying as long as I can, in case you need me. I'm still a bit concerned about being away right now."

She snorted. "Don't be silly. We can't be together for two weeks, anyway. You just do whatever you're doing. But you really should have let me come on alone."

"I hope you're right. I really do. But just in case,

I'm giving you the keys to the camper. If Walter has different ideas about this trip than you do, I want you to sleep in the camper. The tent's fine when I'm around, but if not, you're to use the camper. Promise?" He took her hand and squeezed it.

"Listen. I do not need to be taken care of." She tried to jerk her hand away, but he held on. She stuck out her chin. "Read my lips," she said. "I do not need to be taken care of. I can take care of myself. Got that?"

He ignored her tirade. Instead, he squeezed her hand harder. "Promise that if you're on your own, you'll use the camper."

She opened her mouth, then closed it. At this point, promising seemed easier than continuing to argue, and the camper was much nicer than the tent—not that she'd need to use either. "All right," she said.

He put a key into her hand and closed her fingers over it. She dropped it into her purse and stood up. Jon loaded the luggage into the trunk. Then he put his arm around her, rubbing her shoulder gently. "Listen, I hope you have a good time. I really do. I hope I don't see you for two weeks and that I get you back all tanned and wind-blown and chewed by sandflies."

He leaned over and kissed her. "Good-bye, have fun, and don't forget which feller you belong to." Then he touched her mouth gently, tracing the contours of her lips with a single finger. "And don't come back to the old man with your lipstick smeared."

Judy went into the airport terminal and waited for Walter to clear customs. He appeared all too soon.

He was shorter than she remembered, but was still taller than she was, even in her heels. He was good-looking with his fair complexion, sandy hair, and clear blue eyes. Even though he'd shed his jacket and tie, he still looked every inch the bank clerk who intended someday to be a manager. She kissed him dutifully, the way people kiss distant relatives at family reunions.

"We'll go to the hotel parking lot and leave the car," she said. "The town's small, and I can show you around on foot. Tired?" she asked, remembering her own flight from Bangor.

"A bit, but it doesn't matter."

"You probably should get an early sleep," she said.

He looked at her obliquely. "An early sleep wasn't really what I had in mind for tonight."

A cold wind blew across Judy's mind. The remark was innocent enough. She was letting Jon's attitude get to her, she told herself, suppressing the thought that so far in their relationship Jon had usually been right.

They parked the car. Judy waited while Walter checked in. When he reappeared, they started toward town. Her high-heeled shoes were not going to be comfortable. Since arriving in New Zealand she'd lived in sneakers, with the occasional day in sandals.

Had she dressed up in an attempt to establish distance between them, to make herself more formal and unapproachable?

Whatever. She'd do her best to cope with the businesslike clothing, as she would do her best to cope with Walter. She didn't even enjoy seeing him. She wished he hadn't come. But she'd struck a bargain, and she'd live with it.

She steered Walter through a fantastic mall where the street had been closed to traffic and devoted to shops. There were restaurants, and clothing stores, and drug stores, and boutiques, and gift shops, and about a million shops selling sheepskins.

They pored over pamphlets of tour companies, talking about whether they should raft, or ride horseback, or pan for gold. Judy saw a brochure for gondolas going to a mountaintop restaurant, but on impulse didn't say anything. When they left the mall to wander around the town she managed to stroll in the direction of the gondolas and ducked into the ticket building alone on the pretext that she was looking for a rest room.

When she came out, she had the tickets in her hand, a fait accompli.

"Dinner's on me tonight," she said, "my welcome-to-New Zealand gesture to you."

After an afternoon of sight-seeing, they climbed into a small white gondola and started the ride up the mountain.

The gondola followed the side of a rather steep mountain. Judy could see a hiking trail beneath them. It crisscrossed below in switchbacks, and at times disappeared completely into the adjoining underbrush as it skirted jagged outcroppings of rock.

The scene unfolding below them was spectacular. When they reached the top they made their way to the viewing platform. Judy breathed deeply of the mountain air as she looked down on Queenstown. She could pick out the landmarks she knew. There was the campground—she could see Jon's camper—and the mall, and the post office. The gardens she had strolled through with Jon last night stuck out into the lake, and beyond those she could see the peninsula that was Frankton Arm.

Probably because of the time of day and the cloud formations, the lake itself was an unusual shade of violet, shot with streaks of emerald green. Judy had seen a type of silken cloth that changes color in the light as it moves. This was what the lake looked like, a bolt of violet and emerald silk, shimmering and changing color according to the whim of the light.

Beyond the lake was the jagged mountain range named the Remarkables. All she was sure of was that it would have been a remarkable evening if Jon had been here beside her watching the shimmering violet and green of the silk that was Lake Wakatipu, the lake that breathes.

But she was with Walter. It was Walter who followed her through the smorgasbord line. It was Walter who sat across from her and watched as the violet water deepened to purple while the sunset flamed around them. It was Walter who watched with her while the lights of Queenstown appeared below them and the stars stood out against the velvet sky. Judy kept dutifully pointing to the view, the lights, the Southern Cross, but Walter seemed to want only to look at her.

"Where've you been staying until now?" he asked her.

She tried to sound casual as she answered, "I've been tenting. I'm in the campground that's right here." She pointed. "That one."

"You surely didn't just leave a pitched tent for two weeks."

"Oh, no," she said. "I took it down and booked out."

"I see." He still wasn't satisfied. "What did you do with your things?"

Judy's cheeks began to burn. She hoped he put the flush down to irritation. "I left them with a friend," she said shortly.

"What kind of friend?"

Judy felt cornered. The real answer was *"It's none of your business,"* but she couldn't bring herself to say it. "What does it matter, what kind of friend? Just someone I know who'll still be at the campground when I get back."

She gave up trying to hide her displeasure. "What is this—the Spanish Inquisition?"

He spread his hands in a conciliatory gesture. "Okay, okay. Let's not fight. I was just checking. You're too innocent and trusting. That's all. You could come back to find the friend gone and your belongings with her."

They walked back to the hotel. He carried her bags in from the car and she followed him down the hall to a room. His bags were sitting there, still unopened.

She looked around. "I'd really like to freshen up

before we visit for the evening," she said. "Where's my room?"

"This is your room," he said.

Her voice rose. "Then where's *your* room?"

"This is my room. You don't seriously think I paid this much and came this far just to be trotted through all the shops, do you? Really, Judy."

She grabbed her bags. "I guess you're right," she yelled. "I *am* too innocent and trusting."

He smirked. "And where are you going, Judy? Back to your little tent? The one you've left with a friend? You don't really have anywhere else to go, do you?"

"That's all you know about it," she flung out as she fled before he'd recovered from his shock enough to stop her.

Chapter Seven

Jon sat at the table, books and papers spread around him. He'd asked the young Australian next door to drop over for a drink, so when he heard a tap on the door, he called, "It's open," and barely glanced up.

"I've come for my tent," Judy said.

He reached her in a single stride, and took her in his arms. "What happened?"

He saw her set face, her determined jaw.

"Come on," he said gently as he led her to the sofa. "What happened? Tell me about it."

The sound he heard could only be Judy literally gnashing her teeth.

"You were right," she said. "He booked only one room. He thought I wouldn't have anywhere else to go."

He smoothed her hair and patted her shoulder. "Fooled him, didn't we? Now unclench your teeth and kick off your shoes. I'll make you a cup of tea before I go to the office to get you a spot and pitch your tent.

And don't fret over missing out on the Milford Track," he quipped. "If you're really set on it, we'll do it on our honeymoon."

"No," she said. "Not our honeymoon. I don't want to spoil it thinking of this." She clapped her hand over her mouth and looked at him with round eyes. "Whoops. I can't believe I said that."

He grinned as he swept the books and papers back into the briefcase, then put on the kettle.

"Does he know you're in this campground?"

"Yes, I told him about the tent before I knew."

"Okay, Judy, don't worry about it. There's probably no problem, and I'm sure you could put him in his place even if there were, but, just in case, tonight I take the tent. No argument."

She shivered a bit. "All right," she said. "Just for tonight." She sat down and kicked off her shoes with abandon.

"You'll need this if you're going to chop Walter into little pieces and throw him out into the street, so just drink up." He handed her the mug of that delicious tea. "And now, I think I'd better get over to the office before it closes."

He picked up the tent and left. Judy heard him say to the Australian, who was sitting out having a smoke, "Mind taking a rain check on that drink, mate? Judy's just come in, and she seems a bit upset."

She turned to her tea and sipped it very slowly. It was very hot, but the warmth crept through her, and she began to feel better. She even smiled wryly to herself. She'd wished she didn't have to spend the next two weeks with Walter. Well, she'd certainly gotten her wish. Guilt free.

She'd just slouched down in her seat and closed her eyes when she heard Walter's voice.

"Do you know where the girl who owns that car went?"

"Oh, sure," came the response. Judy recognized the voice of the Australian next door. "She's in the camper van belonging to the American bloke. Right there."

Judy hadn't locked the door. Well, she sure wasn't going to bolt up and do it now, and make Walter think she was afraid of him. However, she wanted to get rid of him before Jon got back. She didn't need to listen to them square off and paw the ground like a pair of bull moose in a bad wildlife movie.

When the door rattled, she snapped her eyes open, sat up, and squiggled her feet back into her shoes.

Walter charged in without knocking. "Left your things with a friend, did you?"

His eyes swept the room. He sneered. "Nice little Judy Gallant. Doesn't smoke, doesn't drink, keeps all dealings with men strictly at arm's length, so to speak. Well, well, well, won't Mama and Papa Gallant and all their friends be interested in knowing the things little Miss snippy, snooty, holier-than-thou Judy Gallant does for fun when she gets to New Zealand. Came here to recover from environmental illness. Hah!"

"Listen," she said, arms akimbo. "I don't have to justify anything to you. I do have environmental illness, although it's much better now. I'm not having an affair. You can believe me or not as you choose, because none of it is any of your business."

Walter backed up a step. "All right. All right. I'm sorry. Okay. I didn't mean anything by it. Why don't we just go somewhere tomorrow and see about getting married?"

She looked at him. "What did I say to you in the Bangor airport?"

"You said I could come."

"Yes. I said you could come if— If what?" She turned her hand palm up and beckoned with her fingers, the way she did when trying to pull an answer from a reluctant student. "If what, Walter? Come on. Your tidy filing-cabinet mind isn't that leaky. What did I say?"

He exhaled. "You said I could come as a friend."

"Right. Do friends play nasty tricks on each other and lie to each other? Do they?"

"For Pete's sake, Judy—"

Suddenly, Jon loomed in the doorway. He paused a second, taking in the scene before him.

"What's going on here?"

"It's none of your business," Judy said.

He looked toward Walter.

"She's right. It's none of your business, whoever you are. But for your information, I'm asking her to marry me."

"A bit late. Judy's going to marry me."

"Excuse me," Judy said. "You two slug it out like the ape men you think you are. I'm leaving." She picked up her tote bag, and slammed out the door. She raced for the tent.

She could still hear them, Walter angry and shouting, Jon's voice calm and reasonable.

Let them work it out. She'd had it with both of them.

Judy awoke at 8:00. She sat up and pushed her fingers through her hair. Somebody was throwing gravel against her tent. Which one of them was it?

"Who is it?" she called.

"Jon. I'm going to make a couple of phone calls. Breakfast's ready as soon as I finish."

"Have you both finished the macho posturing?"

"Let's just say that he responded to an appeal to reason. Now get up. It's time to travel."

She struggled into her green shorts and top, grabbed a towel, and took off for the washrooms.

After she'd had a fast shower and brushed her teeth, she felt much better. The events of last evening seemed somewhere between a nightmare and a silent-movie farce. She returned to her tent, put away her towel and toothbrush, and rolled up her sleeping bag.

When she couldn't procrastinate any longer, she made her way to the camper. Jon was already there. He indicated her place at the table and pushed a cup of tea at her. When she tasted it, she made a face. It must have been half sugar, half water, with a tea bag dragged rapidly through the whole mess.

"Tea? You want me to drink tea, give me tea. Strong and without sugar, please."

"Drink it. It's good for you."

"I don't need something that's good for me. I'm not ill. Just in case you didn't notice."

"But you had a rough time last night."

"That's your interpretation. Frankly, I'm sick of the pair of you. Yes, Walter acted like a jerk. Thank you for setting him straight, but you might have done it without entering into the competitive spirit quite so enthusiastically. I'm not marrying Walter, and I don't remember saying I'd marry you either."

"Ah," he said, grinning his irresistible lopsided grin. "You might not have said so, but you will." He plopped a cup of strong dark tea on the table in front of her. "Is that better? Bacon and eggs?"

She resisted the irresistible grin and said only, "Yes, and yes. That's better. I'll have bacon and eggs."

He dished up breakfast and sat down across from her.

"Okay," he said. "We've got a lot to talk about, but we'll talk on the road. You've got me in a bind for getting to Wellington. I'll grab your bags, and then we'll go. Your car. I've put your tent over the camper cab, and the car's gassed up. As soon as you've finished eating, we'll leave."

"Yes, sir. And just where is it we're going? And why?"

"To Christchurch. That's the next place after Wellington on the itinerary. Walter can't go back until his two weeks are up because of his ticket, and I don't want you to stay here by yourself."

"Oh, yes? I thought you came to all these wonderful

agreements last night. Or you're afraid I'll elope with him while you're gone. Is that your problem?"

Brave words. The truth was, she didn't really want to go another round with Walter. However, there was no need to share that with Jon quite yet.

She picked up her purse, left the camper, and slid into the passenger seat of the car. Jon locked up the camper and put her bags into the trunk. He drove out of town and was on the highway before he started talking again.

"Remember, I've a commitment in Wellington, and I was going to fly?"

"Yes," she said.

"I can't leave you here alone. I don't really think he'd bother you again, but we're not taking any chances."

"Oh," she murmured. "How very macho and protective of you."

Jon went on as if he hadn't heard her. "I've made some fast arrangements. I've friends near Christchurch that run farm vacations. I've phoned, and they'll take you. They're laid-back people who'll leave you alone if you like and will be willing to socialize when you want to do that."

"None of this is necessary."

"Hopefully not. But I still don't think you should stay in Queenstown by yourself."

She sighed. Deep down she agreed with him. "So, we're going to Christchurch. You want to tell me more?"

"All right. The first idea I had was to just take you

to Wellington with me, which we'd have done originally if I hadn't had to bring you down here for the Walter caper."

Judy winced. Whose idea had it been for him to bring her down?

Jon continued, "However, we didn't have time to drive and I couldn't get a second ticket at this point. However, I can get a flight for myself from Christchurch to Wellington, but we can't waste a lot of time on the road. It's a seven- or eight-hour drive, and I want to see you well settled before I leave."

"What about your camper?"

"I'll fly back to Queenstown from Wellington and pick it up and drive to Christchurch. That means I won't see you until late Friday at the earliest."

"Well," she said, still unwilling to concede that his decision was right, "that's the best news I've had in the last two days."

She added, "You don't have to come back to Christchurch. It's all right. I'll be fine on my own."

He swerved the car onto the left shoulder, kicking up a cloud of dust and gravel as he braked suddenly.

He turned to her and grabbed her shoulders. "Now what's this? Why wouldn't I come back to Christchurch?" He was nearly shouting.

"Because you're not my father, and you don't have to take care of me."

His fingers bit into her shoulders. "You addleheaded female, of course I'm going to come back and, furthermore, I'm going to propose to you again. Besides, if you'd been paying attention, you'd have known I have to go to Christchurch anyway. I've got meetings there."

His voice softened, and his hands cupped her face, and his blue eyes were bright with unshed tears. "I love you, Judy, and I am going to marry you. In spite of all the Walters in the world. To say nothing of your own stubborn nature. Now try to snooze for a while. I've got to get Lulabelle or whatever her name is back on the road."

As he drove, he sang to her.

She smiled a bit in spite of herself before she drifted off to sleep.

"How'd you make out with Walter?" she asked when she woke up. "Seriously?"

"Just fine," he assured her. "I told him that his suspicions about us were most incorrect, that I'd never compromised your virtue, not even a little bit, but that I did intend to marry you, and he should butt out."

"And of course he believed you?"

"Absolutely. When I'm serious, I get results. Don't forget that. I talked to your mom, too."

She went cold all over and said, "Oh," in a very small voice. She was afraid to ask.

He grinned across at her. "It's okay. Your mom likes me."

She let her breath out slowly. "What did you tell her?"

"Just the truth, Judy. That usually works out best in the long run. That you're quite safe with me. That I intend to marry you regardless of whether or not you've agreed yet. She sends her love and can't wait to meet me. I thought she should know all this from me instead of from Walter."

"I agree on the last part," she said. "That she shouldn't find out what happened from Walter. The rest, I won't dignify with a comment."

"Why don't you talk to her yourself? We'll stop for lunch where there's a pay phone. Okay?"

She nodded.

Once they'd found a phone, Jon stayed with her until the call went through and then left to give her privacy. In Bangor, it was early evening the previous day, and her parents had just finished dinner.

When she heard her mother's voice, waves of homesickness washed over her. "Oh, Mom," she said. "I miss you and Daddy."

"We miss you, too, dear," Marian told her.

Judy hesitated, and then took the plunge. "I didn't write about him because I wasn't sure you'd understand. We've just been traveling as friends, and that's the way it's going to stay, even if he does keep saying he wants to marry me."

"I know. He told me that. He sounds like a fine man, Judy, but you have to make up your own mind."

Judy walked back to Jon, and he steered her out into the sunlight and toward a tearoom.

"Well?" he asked.

"Yes," she said. "You're right. It's okay."

"Umm." He grinned. "I think I'm going to like your mom."

She looked straight at him. "And you know something else? She didn't say so, but I just suspect she knows more about you than I do."

Judy and Jon reached Christchurch in the late afternoon. Jon introduced her to her hosts, Charlie and Liz Hamilton, then carried her bags up and kissed her lightly at the door of her room.

"I want you to think my proposal over," he said. "I know I've come across pretty heavy-handed, but I'm not really going to drag you by your hair to my cave unless you want to go."

"But who are you?" she asked for the hundredth time.

"Look, I don't want your answer influenced by who I am. I'm respectable. I want you to have these days to think about whether you love me, whether you want to spend the rest of your life with me. If you make that decision, but don't like the answer when you find out who I am, you can always change your mind. You'll know all that before we get married. Okay? Just think about it."

"Yes," she said. "I'll think about it."

"The other thing, Judy, I think you're feeling bad about what happened with Walter, as if it were your fault. It wasn't. Why don't you try writing it all out? What happened and your feelings about it."

"But I can't," she said. "I can't put this in my book. He'd sue me."

"I don't expect you to put it in your book. In fact, you can burn it as soon as you've finished. But do it.

I think it will help you to see the whole thing much more objectively."

He kissed her once more lightly, and was gone.

Her room was delightful, as cool and green as New Zealand itself. The wall-to-wall wool carpet was apple green. Pastel green and pink floral paper covered the walls. The white bedspread on the large double bed was dainty and feminine and ruffled. There were two dressers and a desk. A huge wardrobe filled one corner.

The Hamiltons had obviously renovated the old house. Judy had a private bathroom. The outside wall of her room was glass, covered with filmy drapes which matched the bedspread. A patio door opened onto her own private deck. The room seemed especially spacious to Judy, after weeks of living in a tent and using her suitcases as a closet.

There was a soft tap at the door. Judy opened it. Liz Hamilton stood there, her rosy cheeks and prematurely graying hair making Judy once more homesick for her own mom. Liz stepped inside.

"Hi, Judy," she said, "welcome. We treat guests like part of our family. When you want to be alone, we respect that. When you want to socialize with us and the other guests, that's great. Either way, make yourself at home. Jon did say you were recovering from illness, and might be tired. Would you like a tray tonight and in the morning or would you rather come to the dining room?"

Judy looked at her gratefully, touched by her kindness. "The tray please. That's wonderful of you." She added, "I am tired tonight. The illness Jon referred to was an allergy to something in my school. I'm just about back to normal, but, yes, I guess I do tire a little easier than normal."

When the supper tray came, it included the daily paper and several paperback novels.

Judy appreciated the thoughtfulness. She was tired, what with the past two days being long ones and filled with emotional stress—Walter, Jon. To say nothing of Jon's ultimatum, because although he hadn't called it that, that's what it was. He expected an answer from her when he returned.

The morning tray was delightfully late. When Liz brought it she came into the room and sat down on the bed.

"If you step out the door at the end of your hall," she said, "you'll be on the sun deck over the garage. It's wonderful for sunning. The only other people here at the moment are two older English ladies, and they never go out there. Charlie and I will be busy. There are deck chairs, and you can take a big towel from the bathroom."

"Thank you," Judy said simply. "I think I will."

She lingered over her breakfast, drinking the full pot of tea on the tray, and then unpacked one suitcase, leaving the other for later. Last night she'd just flopped into bed with a paperback novel, and, amazingly, slept well and late.

She put on her swimsuit and padded down the hall with her towel and book.

She chose a colorful lounge from one of the many

grouped on the patio, then applied sunscreen and stretched out on her back, putting up one arm to shade her eyes from the mid-morning sun. The golden rays permeated her very being. It was impossible to be depressed or upset while sunbathing, she thought. The expression "the best of all possible worlds" must have originated when the philosopher was lying in the sun. For years now, medical journals had harped on how bad tanning was for the body, but had the doctors realized how very good it was for the soul?

She didn't pick up her book. Instead she turned over and lay facedown, let her arms drop, and walked her fingers idly on the bright-green indoor-outdoor carpet as she lazily thought about Jon. Her anger with him seeped away, drawn out by the sun's warmth. Her love remained. It was just like a storybook romance. And it had happened to her, plain Judy Gallant from Bangor, Maine.

People say that our emotions betray us, she reflected, but that wasn't the way it had been with her. Her friends, and even her mother, had said of this one and that one, "He's perfect for you, Judy," or, "You can't wait forever, Judy," and, every time, her sixth sense had said, "Ugh."

In Los Angeles airport, when he had said that maybe he had written the song just for her and kissed her on the lips, her intuition had known right away. Her heart had loved him at once, but her mind had betrayed her, saying, *No, no, Judy, love doesn't happen that way. That's just infatuation, Judy. You can't marry a man you haven't known forever.* Well, she'd known Walter forever, and look how that turned out.

She was lucky that Jon hadn't given up on her long ago. But he knew they were meant for each other. He was so much wiser than she was. His mind and his heart were in harmony.

The guessing game of "Who is Jon Brown?" had become a habit with her, but it was no longer an obsession. He obviously was no one sinister. And he had everyone mesmerized. He had charmed even her mother from halfway around the world.

She was dreaming of their promised life in Boston, her writing, his work, the condo, the babies, when she fell asleep under the warm and soothing fingers of the sun.

When Judy awoke from sunbathing on the patio, it was almost 2:00. She returned to her room to find a lunch tray waiting for her. There were very thin tomato and cucumber sandwiches wrapped in plastic to keep them fresh, and a large glass of iced tea with chunks of ice still in it. The glass was frosty with condensation. The tea itself tasted of lemon and sugar. She ate hungrily and then noticed the note on the tray. *Unless you let me know otherwise, I'll bring up tea about seven,* it read.

How thoughtful they were, Judy thought, and how much everybody seemed to like and respect Jon. These people must know who Jon was. They'd probably been warned not to tell her anything, or they probably assumed she was engaged to him. How could she admit she didn't know what her fiancé did for a living and wasn't even sure she knew him by his right name?

Anyway, at this point it would be almost the same as snooping in his briefcase. He would tell her in his own good time, probably as soon as she said, "Yes," which would be the next time he asked her.

She changed into dark blue walking shorts and a white shirt, sat down at the desk, and took out the blank notebook she had packed for writing descriptions of the Milford Track.

"Write it all down," Jon had said.

It was difficult to begin, but once she started it became easier and easier. She decided to write down first in as much detail as she could, what actually happened, starting with the conversation in Bangor airport.

Her feelings, too, Jon had said. Well, she supposed the main feeling was guilt. She paused on that one. Why did she feel guilty? Because it was her nature. Whenever things went wrong she blamed herself. But in this case were there any reasons for her to feel guilty? Yes, he'd spent a lot of money and ended up spending two weeks by himself. But he knew before he came what it would cost. She hadn't led him on. She'd said, "I'll be glad to see you, as a friend." That was true.

Perhaps she could have phoned and said, "I've met someone else. If you still want to come, I'll try to fit you in for lunch one afternoon." That would have been cruel, and it also would have implied that they'd been more than friends before she'd met the someone else.

She wrote it all down, but it seemed very much as if there wasn't a lot for her to feel guilty about. She felt betrayed, of course, because a friend had turned on her, but that wasn't her fault.

And, really, what had happened. Walter had made a pass, and she'd taken off. Later, she'd left the scene of a confrontation between Jon and Walter that probably would have done the Three Stooges proud, although she hadn't stayed around to watch.

After she finished writing, she let her notes sit for a few minutes, and then read them over. She almost laughed. The account read like a minor scene from a badly written novel. She tore the pages up and threw them into the garbage, and started on something more important, like should she marry Jon.

She took a fresh piece of paper and wrote two headings, *no* and *yes*.

She chewed the top of her pen and began to write. *No—I don't know who he is. Yes—I love him. No— He's bossy and arrogant. Yes—I love him. No—He tries to take care of me whether I want that or not. Yes—I love him.*

What it really boiled down to was that she wanted more independence. But she *had* been ill and needed to build up her strength. She *had* found the driving traumatic at first. She *had* gotten herself involved in this situation with Walter. Certainly, she'd have coped with all these things if she'd had to, but having Jon there had sure made it easier.

He'd told her, when she'd still thought the whole thing was a joke, that when they were married, things like whether she wanted to continue working would be up to her. What more could she ask?

After the long lazy day, Judy felt like joining the human race again, and told Liz not to bother with the tray. When she came down to the dining room for the evening meal, there were just six of them at the table—Charlie and Liz, the two English ladies, the young woman who helped in the kitchen, and herself. She was introduced all around.

Yes, she said, she was a friend of Jon's. He'd be coming here in a few days. Nobody seemed to care much, one way or the other.

Then everyone was chattering about the crops and the horses and "Oh, my dear, hasn't shopping become expensive these days?"

Judy discovered that the elderly ladies were English widows on pension doing a six-month tour of New Zealand. They'd had very interesting lives, and she resolved to ask them more about their experiences as army nurses.

The next morning, Liz and Judy went horseback riding through pampas grass with heads that blew like golden flags above their slender stalks, and then up into hills covered with tussocks and sheep. In the afternoon she sunbathed, and lingered over afternoon tea, chatting with the English ladies.

"What a nice young thing," she heard them say to each other as she left the room, "not a bit uppity or patronizing like so many young people nowadays."

Judy smiled to herself. How nice to be approved of.

That evening, after dinner, as everyone ate Pavlova and drank tea, the phone rang. Liz answered it, and Judy heard her say, "She's right here. I'll let you talk to her."

It was Jon. How wonderful to hear his voice.

"How are things?" he asked.

"Wonderful." She lowered her voice. "I did what you said and wrote down all my feelings about Walter. Then I read it, and somehow it all seemed very trivial. It just doesn't seem very important. So then I wrote down all my feelings about you."

"And?"

"Wouldn't you like to know? I'll tell you in person," she added.

"Well," he said, "I have some bad news and some good news. My meetings at Wellington seem to have run into Friday, so I probably won't see you until Sunday afternoon."

"Fine," she teased, "and what's the bad news?"

"Okay, have your little joke. I think you really are fine. The *good news* is on Sunday night I'm going to show you just how much I've missed you."

His voice got husky. "And then, my lovely, on Monday, we'll take horses up into the hills, and over a picnic lunch, I'll propose you a proposal that will knock your socks right off. And this time, I sense that I won't be wasting my time."

"No," she said softly, "you won't be wasting your time."

" 'Bye, darlin'. I love you."

There was an awkward little pause. She wanted to say, "I love you, too," but she had never in her life said this to anybody, and the words stuck in her throat.

Jon ignored the funny little pause and continued, "See you Sunday. Could you check with Liz about the horses and the lunch?" he added as an afterthought before he hung up.

Chapter Eight

Judy asked if the horses were available next day and if Jon and she could have a packed lunch. There wasn't any problem with either, and Liz was delighted that Jon would be in for Sunday dinner (Liz called it "tea"). Liz chose her roast of hogget with special care and decided to have both new potatoes and roast potatoes because she wasn't sure which kind Jon preferred.

Saturday, Judy drove into Christchurch and bought a new dress. Jon would surely take her out to dinner at some point, and she'd brought only one good dress with her to New Zealand. Jon had already seen it more than once.

On Sunday afternoon, she begged to be allowed to help in the kitchen, and made careful mental notes of how Liz seasoned the hogget and how long she cooked it, and how she prepared the pumpkin (which Judy called "squash"). Judy scrubbed the new potatoes and pared the others and washed vegetables and got the strawberries ready for the Pavlova.

"You're a very lucky young woman, you know," Liz said as they worked together in the kitchen. "To be engaged to Jon, I mean."

"Well," Judy confessed, "we aren't really engaged yet." She added, "But I think we will be soon."

Liz stood back and eyed her thoughtfully. "I think he's lucky, too. His friends have worried about him; he's had so many fortune hunters and social climbers after him. I haven't known you long, but you don't seem like that. I feel that you and Jon will be good for each other."

Judy had trouble holding her composure. Fortune hunters and social climbers? Was this tied into his emphasis on her making a decision before she knew his identity? He didn't want her to be influenced by who he was, he'd told her.

Who was this man she was about to marry? She couldn't ask Liz. And how did he know people and have friends, good friends, halfway around the world?

Then she saw the camper swing around the corner. Potatoes and strawberries forgotten, she was outside and running. Jon was out of the camper almost before it rolled to a stop. He reached out and swung her into his arms and kissed her thoroughly, then held her at arm's length and examined her face.

"It's so good to see you, darling."

"Mmm. You too." She stood with her hands linked behind his neck smiling up at him.

He was wonderful during dinner. There was obviously a bond of long standing between him and Charlie and Liz, and they drew Judy into their circle. The old English ladies worshiped him. Judy listened enthralled as they sat after dinner and swapped war stories, the English ladies speaking from first-hand experience, Jon contributing tales gleaned and remembered from his grandparents.

Afterward Judy's heart sang as she walked with Jon around the farm with his arm encircling her shoulders, holding her close. As dusk fell, they gravitated to the porch swing. He held her in his arms, and with his lips explored her hair, her forehead, her eyelids, her ears, and her throat. Her pulse pounded.

He held her closer, and nuzzled the little hollow at the base of her throat. When he kissed the sensitive hollow, she felt as if her heart would burst from sheer happiness.

They drew apart a bit when they heard footsteps coming up the walk. It was the two English ladies. The ladies said "good evening," and Jon and Judy said "good evening." Jon, although he kept an arm around Judy, chatted with them a bit about how nice the evening was and how there was nothing quite like a good walk for the health.

"Well," one said, "we mustn't intrude on you young things."

Jon returned to kissing Judy, as they both listened to the continuing conversation. "Such a nice young couple," one was saying. "She's so sweet. The young man's a bit eccentric, with that funny hat, but so nice.

And do you know, my dear, I heard him check in, and they even have separate rooms. In this day and age, my dear. Isn't that sweet?"

Jon and Judy held their breaths, and when they were sure the women had passed out of earshot, they burst into laughter in unison.

"Such a nice young thing you are," he teased.

"Ah, but I'm not quite sure you're good enough for me," she countered. "Eccentric? I'm not sure I can handle eccentric."

"Nice," he reminded her. "Eccentric perhaps, but nice. Emphasis on *nice*."

"Well, then, perhaps you should propose to one of the English ladies."

"Perhaps I should," he said, and he began tickling her hard until she collapsed laughing into his arms, and they got back to what they both agreed was the main business of the evening.

They couldn't stay there all night. Eventually he had to walk her to her room. She wasn't feeling quite as impulsive as she had the night in Bayside, but still her love drove her, pounding in every cell of her body. He kissed her again at her door, and her arms pulled him against her. She couldn't end this yet. She couldn't let him turn away and leave her. She sought to prolong the moment.

Jon stepped back. "Good night, darlin'."

He kissed her once more, lightly. She'd been dismissed. As she turned into her room, she heard the sound of his footsteps receding down the hall to his room.

She got ready for bed, but she couldn't sleep. It was the same as the other times. What she really felt like doing was working on her book for a few hours. Then she remembered. It was in Jon's camper. Jon had put it there before she went to meet Walter, and she'd forgotten to get it before they left for Christchurch.

She pulled on her robe. She'd wait a few minutes until she was sure she wouldn't meet him—that would be anticlimactic—and then she'd slip out to the camper.

He wouldn't mind. After all, she'd had free run of the camper ever since he'd got it. She took the flashlight she always carried in her tote bag.

If the camper were locked, she'd be out of luck, but it probably wouldn't be.

Quietly she crept along the hall so as not to disturb anyone, and then felt her way down the steps.

The camper wasn't locked. She let herself in and turned on the flashlight. She made her way to the bank of kitchen drawers. The top one was for cutlery. Jon used the next one for miscellaneous.

She opened the drawer and shone her light into it. Yes, her book was there, but there were recent letters on top of it. She reached to move them, consciously resisting looking at them, but, as she lifted them, she couldn't help seeing the top one. She looked more closely. Her father's handwriting was large and spidery. There was no mistaking it.

The letter had no return address. Why on earth would her father write to Jon? He couldn't possibly have known of Jon's existence until the night Jon phoned, and no letter would come that promptly from Maine to New Zealand. Maybe there was someone else who had handwriting like her dad's. She had to know. The letter was addressed to Jon at general delivery, Wellington. It had been opened, which certainly made snooping easier.

She made up her mind quickly, and just as quickly decided to be furtive. Taking the letter, she sat on the floor beside the cupboards.

If Jon happened to come to the camper, she would quickly return the letter, and scramble around the kitchen telling him she thought she'd left her night cream there.

She opened the letter, and held the flashlight directly onto the paper. First she glanced at the end, just to assure herself that it was indeed from her dad. Otherwise, she'd return it unread. It was from him. With trembling hands, she went back to the beginning.

Dear Jon,

I have not heard from you for quite some time. At that time our little project seemed to be progressing nicely. I was worried about the car, and was pleased to hear that you gave her some driving lessons and have helped her in that way. I'm also pleased that you're seeing that she eats properly and gets regular exercise to build her strength up. It certainly is a great relief to both her mother and myself to know that she is being well taken care of and is safe.

So far, Judy has not let us know of your existence. This is a bit unusual, as we have always felt that she was open and honest with us.

My real reason for writing at this time is to see if you need any interim payment. I'm sure you've spent considerable money on groceries, etc. that you would not have for just yourself.

I know that when we planned this, you refused to even discuss reimbursement, but now that you've had time to think about it, hopefully you will be more reasonable. I know that you said you owed me one, but being a person that is naturally tidy about finances, I would feel much better if we kept that part on a strictly business basis. I think you have done more than enough to do this at all, as it must have entailed considerable inconvenience for you. I certainly would not feel right if you were also out of pocket over it.

Therefore, I would greatly appreciate it if you would send me an itemized statement of any money you have spent so far on Judy, as well as a reasonable request for reimbursement for your time.

I trust this finds you well. Both Marian and I greatly appreciate what you have done. I am looking forward to seeing you when you return.

Yours truly,
Harold Gallant

Somehow she managed to fold the letter up again and return it to its envelope. She didn't take her book. The heart for it had gone, and, anyway, if the book were missing Jon would know she'd been in the camper.

It was almost too much to take in, and like a robot she placed the letter back into the drawer, made her way out of the camper and back to the house, moving very quietly, this time not out of consideration but out of fear of discovery. Back in the lounge, she found a couple of paperback books, so that if anyone had heard her in the hall or on the stairs she could say she'd come down to look for a book.

When she finally reached her room, she sat on the bed, dry-eyed, too shattered to cry or lie down or anything. Jon had never loved her. He was baby-sitting her. She was just a *project,* an *inconvenience.* Jon had pretended to love her to keep her around so he could fulfil his commitment to her dad. She was totally betrayed—not only by Jon, but also by her dad. The whole idea had been Dad's. And the most unkindest cut of all, even Mom. Mom had played along with them, although maybe not quite as ruthlessly.

She was just a little girl to all of them, to be baby-sat and to be manipulated into doing what they wanted. Worse yet, it was a business deal. Daddy was prepared to pay him.

She knew something else. She wasn't special or beautiful. "*My lovely,*" he had called her, and she had begun to think that her freckles were appealing and her eyelashes golden and that she was somehow a very special and desirable person. She wasn't. She was just plain Judy Gallant from Bangor, Maine, with freckles, and pale brows and lashes, and carrot-colored hair that framed a pointed little face. She'd been right about herself all along.

How had he fooled so many people, made so many people think of him as an honorable person? She was sure that Charlie and Liz weren't part of any conspiracy. The English ladies and everyone else they'd met along the road had been very impressed by him. Who was he, anyway, that he would do this? Was he a professional guard dog that parents hired when they wanted their little girls protected? But he hadn't wanted payment. And how could she face her parents?

They'd been guilty of the ultimate betrayal. She couldn't just run away from home. Her job was in the Bangor area, and good teaching jobs were very hard to find these days. Besides, her parents were right. She obviously wasn't capable of taking care of herself out in the big bad world. She'd been taken in by the first good-looking smooth talker that came along.

But, most important, she had loved him. He had lied to her, but he had made her love him, and now all the beautiful fireworks had become dead ashes.

She sagged over onto the bed without taking off her robe, and finally the dam broke and she cried, cried until she hiccuped, and then cried some more. At last she fell asleep.

A tap on the door awoke Judy. Jon's voice called to her, "Wake up, darlin'. Today's the day."

Judy was a sodden lump of misery. For a moment she hoped it had all been a horrible nightmare, but she knew it hadn't. She looked at her watch with dismay.

Almost nine. She'd intended to be up and on the road at the crack of dawn to get a good start before anyone missed her. Now she'd overslept, and Jon was banging on the door. Perhaps if she kept very quiet, he would go away for a while, and she could still sneak out without a scene.

She'd decided on a course of action. No way she'd slink home like a beaten pup. Physically, she'd bounced back. Now she'd travel on her own as she'd originally intended to do. First, she'd head back to the North Island. It would never occur to Jon that she'd backtrack to that degree. Even if it did, apparently he had commitments on the South Island, which he'd have to honor.

Originally, she'd intended to leave him a note telling him she'd left and not to look for her. Now she didn't have time for that.

The idea of nobody in the whole world knowing where she was seemed irresponsible, but she had a friend at home, a fellow teacher, she could phone with her new itinerary. Susan wouldn't break a confidence, yet in an emergency, she'd be able to contact Judy.

"Just the truth, Judy," Jon had said. Well, the truth didn't seem to be something he dealt in a lot himself, and didn't seem very helpful here.

Once she got home, she wouldn't so much as mention Jon, and if her mother asked about him, she'd just say he was a friend along the road who'd been good to her, but as far as anything else went it hadn't worked out. Then she'd go back to her own apartment and turn up at home occasionally for Sunday dinner.

So much for the great adventure. She couldn't even take home memories, because the memories were all mixed up with Jon.

He knocked on the door again. "Come on, Judy, wake up. I haven't kissed you for nearly nine hours."

She summoned up her anger. Anger was the only thing that would get her through this.

"Just get out of here," she said. "Get out of my life and stay out." Then she rolled out of bed and started to pack.

Jon froze, hand in mid-air.

Just what was going on here? It didn't sound like Judy at all. Even in the beginning when she'd suspected him of being a reincarnation of Jack the Ripper, she'd never talked to him like that. He told himself that she was probably still half asleep. He'd give her half an hour, and if she still behaved this way, he'd insist on having it out with her.

He saw Charlie down at the corrals putting a Western saddle on one of the big farm horses, so he went on down there.

"Big fellow," he said for something to say as he patted the horse's neck.

"Yes," Charlie said. Charlie was lean and tanned, face lined from the dust and wind of outdoor life. "This is Barney. I'm doing some fencing, and he's strong enough to carry both me and the supplies. He looks a bit sleepy, but he's a good old boy. Anyway, you and your lady love have a monopoly on the riding horses today."

"Um." Jon looked past him to the house. "There's something funny about Judy this morning. She almost bit my head off when I rapped on the door."

"Your filly tends to be a bit skittish, does she, mate?"

"No, that's the thing. She doesn't. Not since she's come to trust me. She's levelheaded, and fun, and a good sport, and she adores me."

"Certainly seemed to last night," Charlie commented dryly.

"And now you'd think I'm Attila the Hun."

"Probably prewedding jitters."

"I don't think so. No," Jon said, "something's wrong, but I can't think of what could possibly have gone wrong between midnight and this morning."

Judy could see the two men leaning on the corral fence. The whole scene could have been straight out of a Western movie—the rail fences, the barn, the riding horses wandering around in the corral, and the old plowhorse tied to the fence. The horse was dark brown, and while his exact ancestry was unclear, the size, the white hairy legs, and the white face suggested more than a touch of Clydesdale.

The men could certainly have been the two lead characters in the movie. Jon would be a perfect hero, handsome in jeans, blue open-necked work shirt, and riding boots, flat English boots rather than the high-heeled pointed ones worn by North American cowboys. The old Australian hat on the back of his head added just a touch of rakishness. Charlie, a bit older, tough as leather, looked the stereotype of the hero's pardner.

Judy turned away from the window. She had to work at keeping her anger white-hot. It was almost unbelievable. He looked so normal, waiting for her down at the corral, so normal and dear and familiar, just as if things were as he said. She bit her lip to hold back the tears and finished her packing, then dressed in white walking shorts and a blue casual top. She checked the room one last time.

Jon saw the movement and swore under his breath. Judy was coming around the corner of the house, sneaking actually. She moved furtively toward her car.

He leaped into action. He threw the reins over the head of the startled Barney and vaulted into the saddle without touching the stirrups.

Jon clapped his heels into the horse's ribs, and Barney broke into a lumbering gallop, probably for the first time in years. Judy heard the hooves and looked up just in time to see the elderly horse bearing down on her. Jon reached down casually and swept her up, folding her facedown over the saddle, between his body and the horn.

She lay as helpless as a bag of grain, flailing legs drooping down one side of the horse, head and arms down the other. The suitcases lay on the grass where they'd fallen. She tried to scream, but the noise came out like a croak from a strangled frog. Jon just laughed.

"It's no use, darlin'. These people all know you're in no danger from me."

Barney ambled back toward the corral.

"Sorry about the fencing, Charlie," Jon said, "but I seem to have commandeered your horse."

"Not to worry, mate. I've got lots else to do around the place." His eyes danced with laughter. "Poor old Barney never dreamed he'd be a steed for a white knight. I'll take care of the suitcases. You two have a nice time."

Furious, Judy screamed at Charlie from her upside-down position, "Do you mean you're just going to let this—this thug carry me off?"

"I never interfere with the path of true love," Charlie replied and turned to the barn to start his other chores.

"You're all sticking together," Judy said. "Why wouldn't he help me?"

"Because he knows you're in no danger. If you were, he'd risk his life to rescue you."

He turned the horse toward the hills, but Barney now refused to move above a walk. Judy was still wedged between the saddle horn and Jon. Her legs dangled helplessly. When she tried to kick, Jon just laughed.

"Let me go!" she demanded, her voice coming out in choking little gasps. "Just let me down now! This minute!"

Jon held her more tightly, but his voice became gentle. "Not until I find out what's going on, Judy. You told me on the phone that I wouldn't be wasting my time if I proposed today. Last night—well, need I say more? And now, here you are trying to run off again and treating me like a leper. Just what has happened since last night?"

"I've changed my mind," she said, her voice muffled in Barney's shoulder. "You told me once that if I really didn't want you, you'd go. Well, I really don't want you. Now go."

"I can't believe that, Judy. My red-haired sweetheart of the Bayside wharf, and of the Los Angeles airport, and of the Queenstown botanical gardens, and of last night. I simply can't believe that."

He pulled her up to a sitting position sideways, held close against his body, turned her head to face him, and brought his mouth down on hers. Barney stopped moving completely and began to graze. Judy went limp as a rag doll. Jon kissed her in all the lovely ways that used to drive her crazy, and that, in truth, still did. He could feel her response in the pulsing beat of her heart against his.

"Satisfied?" she asked scathingly when he finally quit.

"No, I'm not satisfied, and you're not getting off this horse until I get some answers. I won't beat it out of you, I won't hurt you, I won't even kiss you again, and I'll hold you only enough to keep you from getting away. But you are staying on this horse until you tell me why you are behaving this way."

The only response was a flurry of kicks and an attempt to jump off, but her shorts caught on the saddle horn, and she couldn't have got off even if Jon hadn't gripped her more securely. Barney broke into a rough trot.

"That was rather stupid," Jon said in her ear, as he lifted her to sit astride the horse, wedged in front of him. "I'm much, much stronger than you are, and, as you can see, even Barney's on my side. So, my lovely, you may as well tell all."

She shut her lips in a thin tight line and refused to answer.

"Okay, you asked for it." He turned Barney up into the hills, and they rode in silence.

Jon held her lightly with the bridle hand, his other hand hanging loosely by his side. She couldn't get away. Even if she did, what was the point? He'd just catch her again. Even Barney could run faster than she could, never mind Jon.

Finally she burst out, "You won't get away with it. Everybody knows you took me."

"I'm not sure what it is I'm *'getting away with,'* and 'everybody' doesn't really care. Charlie is highly amused, and no one else is paying much attention."

"Then you are in it together," she accused. "It's a conspiracy, and you're all in it together."

He stopped the horse and his arm tightened around her.

"What on earth are you raving about? In *what* together? What conspiracy? Why are you acting so strange?"

She raged on. "You and Charlie and Liz. They must

know about it, too. What's the size of the bill you're submitting?" she threw at him. "All the trouble you've gone to, it'll probably bankrupt Dad to pay it."

"Ah, now we're getting somewhere."

Chapter Nine

W*hat now?* Judy wondered as Jon reined Barney to a halt on the hillside, dismounted, and lifted her down. He threw the reins on the ground and placed a handy rock on one of them. Barney stood resting, head down, his weight thrown on three legs, while one hind leg propped idle.

"Now, let's just sit here and be a bit more comfortable while we talk. And no ideas about running away. I'd love to catch you in a flying tackle."

They sat on the brown grass, Jon on Judy's left. Judy edged away. When Jon tried to take her chin in his hand, she flinched. She would not let him touch her, let him make her forget her suspicions of him. He lowered his hand.

"All right," he said softly, "how did you find out? Did you see the letter from your dad?"

"I wasn't snooping. I just felt like writing last night, after—well, after . . . you know."

"Ah, yes, my lovely, indeed I do know." He chuckled as he bent over and tried to nibble her ear.

She turned her head aside and looked at the trees on her right. "I remembered that I'd left my writing things in your camper, in the junk drawer, so I got a flashlight and went out to get it. I didn't think you'd mind. I've always had the run of the camper. I just went quietly and used the flashlight. Anyway, the letter was on top of my writing supplies, and I couldn't help recognizing Dad's handwriting. Good thing I did, too. When I think of what a fool I've already been— but it's nothing to the fool you'd have made of me if I hadn't seen the letter."

He reached for her hand, but she yanked it away sharply.

He sat a moment with his head bowed over his clasped hands. Then he said, "I'm sorry, Judy. I'm sorry. What can I say?"

"Maybe you might start with the truth." She added bitterly, "If that isn't such a foreign concept you can't handle it."

"Well, Judy, the truth is that I owed your dad for getting me out of a real scrape with the IRS. My accountant from the previous year had been very incompetent. Your dad, as you know, is the best, so I went to him and presumed on family friendship."

"Family friendship? What family friendship?"

"All right. My dad was a university professor before he retired. Your dad was in some of his classes and they became friends. Our families used to visit, but gradually we drifted apart except for Christmas cards, as all of us had busy lives. I'd seen you before, you know," he added. "You were about thirteen with scrapes all over your knees from getting too adventurous with your bike."

She swiveled toward him, analyzing him. She had no memory of having ever seen him.

Jon continued. "Anyway, after the income tax thing, I said, 'I owe you one.' I had no idea he'd collect so soon, and in this way."

She sneered. "And if he'd asked you to commit murder, I suppose you'd have done that too?"

He shrugged helplessly. "Judy—please. He didn't ask me to commit murder. Just to keep you safe. You'd been ill and were still weak as a kitten if you overdid anything. They were worried about you. Honestly, Judy, that is the truth."

"Oh, yes, that was the truth all right. Just keep me safe and break my heart. And why were you really bringing me here today? Were you going to tell me all about it and then say, 'Well, thanks for helping me pay off my debts of honor to your father, Judy. Ciao.' And I suppose you were going to carry a tape recorder in the lunch bag, just in case Dad didn't really believe that you'd done your very best and discharged your obligations as well as earning your honorarium. Is that what you were going to do?"

She'd become very worked up and downright irrational, but she had to stay angry. She wasn't going to cry in front of him. If she could just stay angry enough she could stave off tears.

"It must have been some tax bill," she said, "to go

to all that trouble for nearly three months just out of gratitude for having gotten out of it."

The facade crumbled. "What am I going to do about our family?" she whispered, almost to herself. "How can I behave like a loving daughter to Mom and Dad after this? Whatever am I going to do?"

She saw pain knife across his face, but when he spoke he was the old Jon Brown, confident and debonair.

"Well, Judy," he said, as he chewed on a grass stem he'd picked, "I actually was bringing you up here to propose, regardless of what you seem to think. Why don't you just go ahead and marry me? Then we'll face your parents together. That sounds like a good solution for you."

"Oh, really! Well, let me tell you, Jon Brown, you needn't think that marriage to you is such a grand prize that every woman in the world would suffer any indignity to get it. I'd—I'd—I'd rather marry Walter," she finally flung out.

He laughed. The arrogance of him. He sat there and laughed at her.

"And what's so funny?" she demanded.

"You are. What a little fishwife I'm taking on. And as for Walter—I've already told you why I feel he wouldn't be suitable."

He caught her hands and refused to let go, "Now just listen to me for a minute. Yes, it did start out that way. I should tell you that it was a mistake, that I never should have agreed to it, that I'm sorry, but I can't honestly say that. I'm sorry you found out about it this soon and in this way, but if I hadn't done what your father asked, I'd never have met you, and that would a been a far more serious mistake.

"Now, I had a sort of tough job. We knew you'd react this way if you found out, so I had to think of something to keep you interested enough to let me hang around. I settled on curiosity. I thought with the songs and the eccentric behavior, you'd let me hang around just to see what would happen next. I'm not sure exactly when it started to change. At first, I think when you took off on me. Part of my upset then was the feeling of responsibility, but part how I felt about you. But then on the Bayside wharf—I cared for you so much at that moment, Judy, that my words were sincere at the time I said them.

"I sat in the dark at the beach pondering how I'd get out of it if you interpreted my comment as a proposal of marriage and said yes. Then I saw you swimming in the moonlight and wasn't sure I wanted to get out of it anymore. At this point, I was all mixed up. I really liked you. I'd started to love you. I'd promised your parents I'd take care of you. Falling in love hadn't been part of the bargain."

He paused. Judy stared stonily into space.

"Well," she said, without looking at him, "go on."

"Yes." He continued, "Then when you told me that Walter was coming, it seemed the perfect time to cool things down, but I just couldn't. That was the decision I was making at Rotorua when I told you I needed half an hour alone. I could no longer drift and procrastinate about the way I felt. I knew that at that point

I either had to let you go forever or play for keeps, and I made the decision to play for keeps."

"Thanks loads. Apparently you're the only one entitled to decisions. I just go along and do as I'm told. Anyway, you made this marvelous *decision*—"

He winced. "It wasn't a very difficult decision, Judy. As soon as I faced thinking about it seriously, I knew I loved you—in all ways. As my love, as my best friend, as my companion. I couldn't face the rest of my life without you. And when I talked about getting married then, I meant it—really meant it.

"And then, after the Walter episode, although it didn't seem possible, I loved you even more, beyond what I'd ever imagined. I do love you, Judy, and I want to marry you. Please, Judy, marry me. Someday we'll talk about this as a great joke. Please."

"Harrumph," she said. "Some joke. With me as the butt of it. And what are you doing here to begin with? Did Dad pay you enough to make this trip just to, um, 'take care' of me?"

"No," he said. "I was coming. Your dad just encouraged you to come at that particular time, and bought your ticket, and sat down and helped you plan your itinerary after he knew mine."

She remembered the sudden capitulation about the trip. How her dad bought her the ticket for Christmas and then sat down with her to help her plan her itinerary. At least that's how it seemed then. Now she realized that Dad had done all the planning.

Jon went on, "I come to New Zealand every time I

can find an excuse. I just felt it was time that I wanted to come again."

The lies he could spin. Did he have them preplanned as exigency measures, or did he actually come up with them as he went along?

"Well," she said, "that's a fascinating story. You really should write fiction. Or perhaps you do," she added. "Please continue."

"And I have a lot of good friends here, people like the Hamiltons, that it was time to visit."

"Oh, yes," Judy said, "you just decided to spend six months in New Zealand because you felt like dropping in on friends. I'll watch for the book when it hits the stands. Really well-written, it should be a best-seller."

The grin had left his face. Maybe he'd finally realized she might not be that easy to get around this time.

"Judy," he said, a bit desperately, "forget your parents. Forget Walter. Forget the dreadful way in which this whole thing started. Marry me. Please, darling. I love you to distraction."

She said, "Are you sure you have the tape recorder running so that Dad will know it wasn't your fault when I leave you, this time so you can't find me?"

He paused a moment. She'd never seen Jon taken aback before, at a loss for words, uncertain what to do next, and she told herself she gloried in it. Then he seemed to reach a decision.

"All right, my lovely," he said as he pulled her to her feet. "It's back on Barney. I know you love me. In fact, we settled that on the Bayside wharf, but I've hurt you, and you don't trust me any longer. You don't think I really love you or want to marry you. You think that for some demented reason I've come here just to collect the fantastic wealth your father is paying me for keeping an eye on you. If you stop to think about it, that's a far crazier story than the one about dropping in on friends."

He swung into the saddle, then reached down and clasped Judy around the waist with both hands.

"Up you come, darlin'. Now if you just sit sidesaddle with your right knee hooked around the horn, I think you'll be more comfortable. I won't let you fall."

Barney showed more enthusiasm for the downward trek until Jon forced him past the road to the ranch and turned him toward Christchurch.

Judy came back to life. "Where are you taking me?"

"Just to allay your fears and suspicions."

The ranch was only a few miles out of town, but at Barney's reluctant pace the journey seemed to take hours. True, the sidesaddle position was more comfortable, but Judy was still tired and hot, angry and embarrassed. The embarrassment didn't ease when they reached the edge of the city and people started looking at them.

Finally they came to a building with a sign reading, CUNNINGHAM, CUNNINGHAM, AND CUNNINGHAM, BARRISTERS AND SOLICITORS. Jon dismounted. He tied Barney to a parking meter and carefully dropped in two twenty-cent pieces. Then he lifted Judy off the horse but kept a tight hold on her hand.

Probably, here, if she screamed and fought and ran,

she could escape. But here she was obviously in no danger, and, she admitted to herself, she was getting too curious to leave at this point. She wouldn't admit to herself that she hoped Jon could prove he really loved her.

"Come on," he said as he dragged her into the law office, and, after chatting briefly with a receptionist, into one of the offices beyond. Judy waited red-faced for the secretaries to break into peals of laughter, but they didn't. They behaved as if having a man in jeans and an old fishing hat tie a horse to a parking meter, put in money, and drag a dusty, bedraggled young woman into the office was an everyday occurrence.

The lawyer, young and blond and clean-cut in his smart navy-blue walking shorts, white shirt, and tie, wasn't ruffled either. He waved them to seats, then took a second look, and stood up with outstretched hand. "Jon! Good to see you. What can I do for you, mate?"

Oh, no. He was in on it, too. Surely her father wasn't paying off all of them just to ensure she'd be well and properly baby-sat in New Zealand.

"Well," Jon said, "as Charlie Hamilton would say, 'my filly's a bit skittish.' And I'd like you to draw up a bond to ease her mind. If I, after she accepts me, refuse to marry her, if I have any other wives or children, legitimate or otherwise, if I am or ever have been involved in activities criminal or unacceptable to normal society, or if I ever have been or presently should be in a mental institution, I will forfeit to her the sum of fifty thousand dollars. There. Put it in whatever legalese makes you happy, but that's the gist of it."

The lawyer looked at him in disbelief.

"There's nothing illegal about that, is there?" John said.

"Oh, no, no, no. Not at all." Cunningham put his professional face back on. "It's a bit irregular perhaps, certainly unusual, but no, no, I certainly can't see why it should be illegal."

"Could I use your phone to get a cab? I don't have fifty thousand dollars in my pockets, and I've been on this wretched horse so long now, I'm not riding him to the bank."

The lawyer pushed his telephone across the desk.

"And," Jon added, "whatever you do, don't let her take off while I'm gone."

Cunningham drew himself up stiffly. "Jon," he said formally, "this is a free country, and the young lady appears to be of age. I can't and won't keep her here against her will."

"Oh," Judy said, "don't worry. I'll stay. I wouldn't think of leaving before I see what dull and boring entertainment you have planned for me next."

A flicker of amusement crossed the face of the young lawyer, but, once Jon had left, he went through the formal procedure of getting Judy's name and address, and put his secretary to work drawing up the document. No tremor in her professional facade betrayed that this was more unusual than the typing of a routine real-estate transaction.

Cunningham surveyed Judy with interest. She knew

she looked a mess. Her shoes were scuffed, her shorts and top were rumpled, and she was generally tired and dirty and uncombed.

Finally he cleared his throat. "Miss Gallant," he said, "I'm not sure just what is going on here, and it isn't my business. I don't know Dr. Brown that well, but I do know he is highly respected, and, in spite of being, shall we say, somewhat unconventional, is a very fine man. What I'm trying to say is that if he really wants to marry you, I wouldn't play hard to get too long if I were you."

He paused, looked her over from her dusty hair to her wrinkled clothes, and added reluctantly, as if he had tried to suppress the comment and couldn't, "I'm sure you have many charms that are not obvious at the moment."

She should have been insulted. Instead she was touched. Had she finally, unlike Diogenes, found an honest man? She could no longer hold back tears.

"I know I'm a mess." She swiped at the tears rolling down the side of her nose. "And I'm so mixed up and confused. He keeps following me around and serenading me and proposing to me, and I don't even know who he is. You called him Dr. Brown. I'm not even sure if Jon Brown is his real name. And then last night I learned something which made me think he was just watching out for me as a job, a job he was being paid for—"

She couldn't bring herself to tell this stranger that her own parents were the ones paying him. "But now he's posting this fifty-thousand-dollar bond. I've steeled myself all morning to hate him and be aloof and controlled. I don't know what to do." She swallowed and sat up straight. A last angry tear rolled down her cheek.

The young lawyer sent his secretary out to make tea. Then he came around his desk to hand Judy paper handkerchiefs and pat her shoulder.

"Go ahead," he said. "Have a good cry and get it all out. It'll help."

"No, it won't," she said with a final sniffle. "I tried that last night, and it didn't help a bit. How long will it be?" she asked. "There's no way *he's* going to see that I've been crying."

"It'll be a while," he assured her. "The bank will have to make some phone calls, and he'll probably have to get some sort of short-term loan until he can get money wired from America. And it's Sunday evening there. He's well enough known that he'll manage, but it'll take a while. It's easier than it used to be, but you still can't stick a card in a machine and get out fifty thousand dollars."

She dabbed at her eyes and blew her nose. This was the first time she'd had anybody to share her problem with.

"Who is he?" she asked. "You know."

"Well," he said, "I guess I've already breached client confidentiality without realizing it, so I can't say any more. But I can tell you this. He is very respectable. I don't know why he's taking this approach, but you needn't fear to accept him. I think the question is, do you love him?"

She sat a moment, asking herself the same question. "Yes," she said firmly, "I do. I love him so desperately I can't stand it. The question is, can I trust him?"

He handed her more tissues, and leaned back against the desk, facing her. Finally he said, "I think he's just bet you fifty thousand dollars that you can trust him, Ms. Gallant. Whatever game he's playing, you can trust him. And now, you still have quite a bit of time left before he comes back, but my secretary's due with tea any moment. So I'd suggest you have a cup of tea, and after that you can use our washroom to freshen up a bit, and be ready to meet him, chin up, when he returns. Right?"

She gave a wan smile. "Right."

He reached out and touched her chin with a gentle fist. "Atta girl. Good on ya."

The secretary came in with a big tray holding a pot of tea, three cups, sugar, cream, and a plate of biscuits. She poured tea and took her own cup to her desk and went back to work.

By time Jon came back, Judy had had tea and had washed and felt much better. Jon handed a slip of paper to the lawyer and said, "Here's a certified check for fifty thousand dollars. Now if Judy can just have a copy of the bond, we'll go."

"I don't want your fifty thousand dollars," she muttered between clenched teeth.

"Don't worry, darlin'," he said. "You won't get it. If you turn me down, it doesn't count."

"Would you like me to give Miss Gallant a drive back to the farm?" the lawyer asked.

Judy put her chin in the air. "No thanks," she said. "I appreciate the offer, but I guess I'd best go home with the feller that brought me." She laid her hand gently on his arm, and said softly, "Thanks for everything," before she turned and, with Jon, walked out to Barney.

The ride back was silent, and when they reached the farm, Jon said, "Why don't you have a long bath and a nap. I'll wait until after dinner before I start badgering you again."

She washed her hair in the shower, and then she filled the tub with bubble bath and hot water. It was heavenly. She lay back and deliberately blanked her mind. This was the first real bath she'd had in New Zealand. It had been nothing but showers in campgrounds. In the few days she'd been here she'd continued showering, mainly from habit. She'd almost forgotten the luxury of lying back in a hot bath submerged in a cloud of frothy bubbles.

Yes, she'd have to deal with Jon later. She'd probably have to come up with some sort of answer tonight, but she suspected she'd do better to put it on hold for the moment, rather than chase it around in the squirrel cage of her mind.

When she finally left the tub, wrapped in a towel the size of a bedsheet, her room was warm from the afternoon sun. She turned back the blankets and lay down, still wrapped in the towel. Before she knew it, she was sound asleep, mind blank, relaxed in the drowsy warmth.

The sun was low and the room less bright but still warm when she heard a rap on the door.

"Yes," she said, knowing who it would be.

"May I come in?"

"No, not yet. I'm not dressed."

"That's fine. It's almost dinnertime. The deck's warm and pleasant. Do you want me to bring up trays for us there rather than going down?"

"Yes," she said. "Give me twenty minutes."

There was no point in stalling, but she still had no idea what she was going to say. Stubbornly she clung to her belief that a woman had a right to know whom she was marrying before she said yes no matter how highly recommended he was by his friends and his lawyer. Then, too, he'd deceived her horribly. Who was to say he wasn't deceiving her again? Other than his lawyer.

The suitcases she'd dropped outside had been carried in during the day, and now sat in a neat row along the wall. She rummaged through the large one and found the white dress and sandals she'd worn in Bayside. True, the dress was more than a little rumpled, and her hair was frizzy because she'd just towel-dried it before lying down, but she felt and looked fresh.

When she reached the deck, Jon was already there. He'd actually changed into dress pants, and the old hat was nowhere to be seen. She'd seen him dressed up only rarely, although she knew very well that once he was out of her sight he changed into a suit and tie for his meetings. He was sitting sideways on one lounge chair and was using another, cushion removed, to hold the dinner tray.

"Eat first, darlin'," he said, indicating the space beside him, "and then we'll talk."

Judy was famished, and hungrily tackled the slices of cold hogget, the potato salad, and the strawberries and cream. Just like a condemned man at his last meal.

"That was good," she said. "You know, this is the first food I've had since last night except for a couple of biscuits that your lawyer fed me with tea."

"You're kidding." He took her hand. "I'm sorry I was so thoughtless. I had a good breakfast, and I guess I just didn't think."

"It doesn't matter. I couldn't have eaten anyway."

He poured the tea, and then took both her hands in his. Hers were icy cold, although the evening was warm and still. He released her hands and drew her into his arms.

"Judy," he said, "I've really messed things up, but I do love you. I love you so much that I would either die for you or kill for you if I had to. Marry me, darling, please."

She nestled in closer to him, but she just said, "Tell me who you are, Jon. If you really love me as you say, you can surely do that."

"At first I kept who I was from you just in case knowing would cause you to make the connection with your father."

She sighed. "Yes, I understand that, but you could surely tell me now."

"Of course I could, but having gone this far, I've

sort of decided I'd like you to marry me for what I am, not who I am."

"What's the difference? If I'm a gold-digger, I've already discovered that you're rich, and I've heard several comments that imply you're important. And if I wanted I could say yes now with the intention of changing my mind if you weren't rich or important enough."

"All right." He sounded tired. "Just confess you love me."

"You said you already knew that," she countered. "You said you knew that when you kissed me on the Bayside wharf."

"Yes, and I know it by what you wore tonight, but I've got to hear you say it. You've never told me that you love me. You've admitted that I drove you crazy, but you've never once told me that you love me." He moved one hand restlessly up and down her bare arm. "Tell me, Judy. Say you love me. Tell me, Judy."

She couldn't stand it any longer. "All right. I love you!" She shouted it at him. "I love you! I love you! There! Are you satisfied now? I love you!"

He drew her close. "Thank you, Judy. I'm satisfied." He added with a grin, "And Charlie and Liz are satisfied, and the two English ladies are satisfied, and Barney is satisfied, and probably half of Christchurch is satisfied, but at least if you try to deny it, I won't be short of witnesses."

She began to cry in great gulping sobs. Jon raised her head and gently brushed a finger under her eyes.

"Why are you crying, Judy?" His voice became

tender. "It's one of life's most beautiful moments when you realize you love someone who loves you. Don't cry, darling. It's a time for happiness."

She sobbed more loudly into his shirtfront.

"Judy, come on. You never cry. I've never seen you cry before."

"You don't see everything. I cried all night last night because I really loved you, and I thought you were just making a fool of me." The very thought of it sent her into fresh paroxysms.

He held her more tightly. "Judy, I'm sorry. I really am. I know I'm an insensitive clod," he added, "but I really do love you, and now you've admitted you love me too, everything's going to work out." He gave up on trying to soothe her and just said, "Go ahead, get it all out," and held her.

Eventually she was cried out, and gave a couple of final shudders and looked up at him. "Jon, I do love you. I really do."

He held her silently, resting his cheek against her hair.

At last she said, "And now, do I get some answers?"

"You can if it's really important to you. But I'd sort of planned if you accepted me today to have the big unveiling in spectacular form tomorrow. Can you wait until tomorrow? Your curiosity's kept you around so far. Can you bear to forego what comes next?" He added quizzically, "It'll be good material for the book."

She grinned at him. "Let's go for it," she said. "Who knows what fascinating experience lurks in wait for me that I'll miss out on if I say no? So what happens tomorrow?"

"That's better. Now, tomorrow I want you to go to the auditorium at the college in Christchurch at ten-thirty. You'll find out then who I am. Then I'll make reservations for us for lunch. If you don't like what you see at ten-thirty, and don't show up for lunch, I'll never bother you again. Just leave a message, so I'll know there was no mistake and won't wonder whether it was like one of those novels where seventeen people get killed because the maid put the milk bottle in the wrong window. But you must turn up at the college at ten-thirty. Will you?"

She nodded. "You'd better tell me where the college is and go over the map with me," she said.

"I will, tomorrow morning."

"And you know what, Jon Brown?" She wound her arms around his neck.

"What, my lovely?" he asked as he nuzzled her hair.

"Why don't you just shut up and kiss me?"

And he did, very deliberately, and when he had kissed her as thoroughly as their unmarried state and good taste would allow, he held her very close while he sang.

"I wooed you in Auckland, I'll wed you in
   Christchurch
 I wooed you in Auckland, I'll wed you in
   Christchurch
 I've chased you all over the New Zealand coast.

I love you when you're crying, I adore you when laughing,
But when you told me you loved me, I loved you the most."

Chapter Ten

Next morning, Judy pushed a piece of toast around her plate as she watched Jon wolf bacon and eggs.

"We may as well go together as far as the hotel," Jon said. "I've a room there for tonight, and you can use it to change for lunch. It was booked some time ago," he added. He looked at his watch as he prepared to sit back with a second cup of coffee. "It's only eight. We still have an hour."

"What should I wear?" She'd worn jeans and a comfortable sweatshirt down to breakfast.

"A simple skirt and blouse for the college, and something quite nice for lunch."

She went to her room. Her clothes were still in the suitcases where she'd packed them yesterday with more haste than taste. Just as quickly she rummaged through them now. For the college, she chose a straight navy-blue skirt and a plain white shirt, and for lunch the new dress she had bought in Christchurch— a shimmering silk the color of new spring leaves.

167

She slipped down to the laundry room and ironed both outfits.

Back in her room, she reminisced as she dressed. The choices had narrowed in the "Who is Jon Brown?" game. He was obviously giving a lecture and was probably a writer. He'd already admitted to being one of her dad's clients, and writers were Dad's specialty.

But then, her father's clients weren't restricted to publishers and professional writers. Other types of people frequently had nonfiction books published. Jon could be a well-known scientist or perhaps even an astronaut.

He could be a teacher or professor. An ordinary teacher or professor wouldn't be on a lecture tour halfway around the world, but one that published research might be, and might also be a client of her father's. Maybe the possibilities hadn't narrowed that much after all.

She laid the green dress on the bed so as not to wrinkle it. Her white high-heeled sandals would go with both the dress and the outfit she intended to wear to the college.

She packed the silk dress carefully in a plastic bag, gave herself a last once-over in the mirror, and went downstairs.

Jon was waiting for her, still in the faded cutoffs and Australian hat.

So, he was playing the game out to the very end.

They walked to the car together. He hung up her

dress, then opened the passenger door for her. The back of the car was crammed with his luggage.

He reached out and took her hand and said huskily, "I guess you know this is D-day, don't you?"

She nodded. There was a lump in her throat for the golden days behind them. Life ahead might be, would be, very good, but she could never again dance on the Bayside wharf with the man she knew as plain Jon Brown.

He started the car and for a time drove in silence.

"In another hour, you'll know," he said finally. "And if you want my driver's license, junior high report card, dental X-rays, and three references, you may have them. But if you don't turn up for lunch, or if you do but still say no, that's it."

"Yes," she said, "I know." Her face crumpled.

He glanced sideways at her. "For heaven's sake, darlin', don't cry."

Her voice broke. "I won't cry, but it is sad. It was a beautiful idyll, a sort of never-never land."

He couldn't speak for a moment, and when he did, his voice was unsteady. "Just as long as you know the rules, my sweetheart of the Bayside wharf. Oh, never mind."

He swung the car to the side of the road, shut off the motor, and took her into his arms. "One more kiss with plain Jon Brown, darlin'. And let's make it worthwhile—the one for the road."

When they stopped at the hotel, Jon spread out a city may and showed Judy how to get to the college.

He traced in the route for her. "You shouldn't have much traffic at this time of day. If you start at ten, you'll be fine."

Then he described where to park and how to find the right building and wrote the directions out for her in the corner of the map. When they walked into the hotel, he held her close as if he too regretted the ending of this chapter in their lives.

"Ms. Gallant will be using my room a bit later," he said to the desk clerk. "Would you give her a key, please?"

And then with a final squeeze he dismissed her. "Go have a cup of coffee while you wait. I'll see you in an hour."

She made her way into the restaurant a bit disconsolately. There was little doubt that she would soon be engaged to someone very exciting, but Jon Brown was gone. He'd shuffled her off, out of the way, while he changed into someone expensively dressed and very important, leaving the trappings of plain Jon Brown discarded and forgotten on the floor of a hotel room.

She tried to drink her coffee, but it stuck in her throat. She tried to think ahead, but the memories got in the way—the Los Angeles airport, the night curled up in his arms while they flew south from Honolulu, the white beach north of Auckland, the magic moments when they had danced in the moonlight on the Bayside wharf. There were too many memories. She couldn't count them all, but she knew she must stop thinking of them, or she'd damage her eyeshadow.

She was glad when her watch read 10:00, and she could step out of her nostalgia and into her future. His luggage was no longer in the car, and neither was her dress. His directions had been explicit. She drove straight to the college, parked the car, and found the room. She was still early and the auditorium was three-quarters empty.

She made her way into a middle row, sitting next to a couple of young women dressed in black pants and sweaters.

Students continued to file in, a mixture of girls like the ones beside her and girls with fresh cotton skirts and tops and neat hairdos. There were boys in shorts and boys in jeans and boys in dress pants, some with beards and some clean-shaven.

The chatter which had been building up subsided as three men walked onto the stage, two obviously teachers at the college, and the other one was Jon. It was difficult to recognize him as her Jon. The unruly curls had been forced into respectable waves, and he wore horn-rimmed glasses. He was dressed in a dark suit, a shirt so white it dazzled, a conservative tie, and highly polished black oxfords.

It was Jon, but there was little resemblance to the man she knew and loved. This man looked distinguished and scholarly. There was nothing left of the rover. Something else niggled at her, some little image in her mind that told her this face was familiar—not as Jon, but as someone else, someone who was distinguished and scholarly and almost famous.

And then, as Jon and one of the other men sat down,

the first man began speaking, something about how fortunate they were to have as a lecturer the noted professor of literature and best-selling novelist, Dr. J. Marlowe Brown from Harvard University, better known to his readers by his pen name, Jonathan Marlowe. Judy went numb. She loved his books, all of them. She'd read each one at least twice. That was why he looked familiar—his picture had been on the book jackets, and in newspapers.

Dr. J. Marlowe Brown—of course, Jonathan Marlowe Brown. While she'd been mentally running over names of football players, hockey players, and entertainment celebrities, and keeping in mind that his name might not even be Jon Brown, the truth had been here all the time. His name really was Jon Brown, and he was in New Zealand on a lecture tour.

She'd once accused him of talking like a college professor when he forgot he was masquerading as a hick, and just yesterday she'd accused him of being a writer. Well, he was both a professor and a writer, and he'd been chasing her all over New Zealand, serenading her every day and twice on Sundays.

She knew she should listen to the lecture. The students were leaning forward, listening intently, and he seemed to be talking to them as casually as he talked to her. It was something about their preparing to be teachers, and students shouldn't hate literature. After all it was life, and if they remembered it was life when they taught it, students wouldn't hate it because nobody hated life. But all she could think about was how good-looking he was and how incredible it was that he loved her—Judy Gallant from Bangor, Maine.

Apparently she wasn't the only one doing more looking than listening. One of the girls beside her whispered to the other, "What a hunk. I wonder what having him love you would be like." When Judy gave them a startled look and turned red, the girl taunted her, saying, "What do you think, Miss? What do you think having him love you would be like?"

Judy answered stiffly, "I'm sure I wouldn't know," and endured their giggles.

If they only knew. She tried to turn her attention back to what Jon was saying. He finished his lecture by quoting a poem about red and white roses, and different kinds of love. When Jon explained that this interpreted feelings about real life he seemed to talk directly to her.

There was a pause and a lot of clapping, and then he invited questions from the floor. There were a number, some of which led to animated discussions. He was a good teacher, Judy thought, a fantastically good teacher.

The girl next to Judy raised her hand, and when Jon acknowledged her asked, "Are you married?" The other students were annoyed, but Jon lifted his hand, and they fell silent.

"No, I'm not," he said, "but I hope to be soon. Sorry about that, Miss, but there's this lovely young woman I've been chasing all over the country, serenading her everyday and twice on Sundays and proposing to her almost as often. She should be here this morning."

He looked out over the crowd. "Are you there, Judy?" She could recognize Jon, her Jon—not this stranger—in his voice, and she raised her hand shyly. "Okay, darlin', stand up so these folks can see you."

She thought of the earlier snickers of the girls beside her, and stood up boldly.

"Thanks, darlin'." His glasses had slid down on his nose. "You'll get your next proposal over lunch."

She made a megaphone of her hands. "I'll be there," she yelled. He nodded approval as he poked at his glasses with a forefinger and turned his attention to the next question. It was time for her to go back to the hotel and get ready for the luncheon date.

On a playful impulse she turned to the young woman beside her. "I'll let you know in a few days if you like."

"Know what?"

"What it would be like to have him love me. I'm going to marry him, you see."

She left the girl open-mouthed, and edged past the rest of the people in the row. When she got out, she almost ran to her car and drove back to the hotel.

The trappings of Jon Brown were not left scattered on the floor. The room was tidy. Only the old Australian hat was in evidence. It was tossed casually on the bed, beside her green silk dress, which he'd carefully laid out. She picked up the hat almost reverently and placed it against her cheek for a moment. Then she held it in her left hand while she caressed the brim with her right, lingering a moment on the red fishing lure pinned to the upturned side. Reluctantly she laid it back on the bed and turned to the dress.

Although she was only five-foot-four, she had a good figure. The wide belt on the silk dress set off her slender waist. Her legs were long and shapely, flattered to look even better in the high-heeled shoes. Her large gray-green eyes were the best feature in her oval face, and the eye makeup combined with the color of her dress made them look clear green today. Her red-gold hair shone, and she felt now that her eyebrows and lashes were truly golden. Jon could be justifiably proud of her.

And she knew now that she was a special person. She had won the heart of Jonathan Marlowe, the Jonathan Marlowe who had beautiful blonds tripping over each other trying to get his attention. With a surge of confidence, she moved downstairs.

The hostess took her to a table tucked away in a back corner. She suspected that Jon had requested privacy when he booked the table.

He came in and slid into the chair opposite her.

She looked up and smiled tentatively. "Do we have to talk about the weather as usual until we have tea?"

"No," he said, "no, not if you don't want to. It will probably take a while, so I may as well start. I've already ordered, so lunch should be here shortly."

There was a pause.

"I didn't know you wore contacts," she said to fill the silence.

He laughed. "I don't." He handed her the glasses. "They're just clear glass. See. When I first got into this business, I was very young to be a professor, and I thought they made me look more distinguished. And later—well, later, I guess I couldn't drop them because they'd become part of the image."

He reached across the table, took her hand and squeezed it. "Don't be nervous. Nothing's changed. I'm the same person. And you're beautiful today, Judy. Stunning."

"Jon," she said. "Why? Why did you go through all that trouble with the horse and the bond? I understand why you couldn't tell me all along, but once I'd seen Dad's letter, why didn't you just tell me the next morning?"

"Think about it. What would your reaction have been if, in the midst of thinking I was lying about absolutely everything, including my love, I had said, 'Oh, yes, by the way, who I really am is Jonathan Marlowe, best-selling novelist'?"

She blushed and looked down. "I guess I'd have thought you were lying," she said.

"Then, too," he added, laughing at her just a bit, "I thought it would make a wonderful story for our grandchildren. And," his voice softened, "before you settle down to married life, I wanted you to live your own real-life romance novel.

"Now," he continued, as he released her hand and leaned back in his chair, "I do have some explaining to do. I have a Ph.D. in English Literature, and, as you now know, got a job teaching at Harvard. I always wrote a fair number of articles, edited anthologies, that sort of thing, but there's not enough money in that to complicate life and taxes. I also spent a year in New Zealand, teaching some courses at the university here in Christchurch, and that's how I acquired the wonderful friends I have here.

"Then, I decided to try my hand at writing a novel, and another, and another, and was lucky enough that they were all best-sellers—hence my connection with your father. I've already explained all that. That's why I agreed to keep an eye on you while I did a lecture tour and collected background material for a new book."

He grinned at her. "Yes, Judy, I'm writing a novel based on this trip too. We'll have to compare notes when we've both finished."

He continued, "He was very adamant that you not know what I was up to. That's why I behaved as I did—hoping you'd be so curious you'd want to see what happened next instead of just going to the police for a restraining order. Try not to be too hard on your mum and dad, Judy. They did this because they love you and were really worried about you.

"Anyway, that's how it started. Then, when I saw you in Bangor airport, you were so lovely I was attracted to you at once. When I got to know you, you became very precious to me. I fought it for a long time, partly because of the, uh, conflict of interest, and partly because I wasn't sure J. Marlowe Brown, eligible bachelor, was quite ready to be caught. I never really had a chance in the face of your basic goodness. Face it, Judy. It was ordained."

The waitress brought two plates of seafood casserole, but they sat at the side of the table, ignored.

"So there you have it. The next three weeks I'm in the Christchurch area, which will give us time for the wedding, and then we'll travel around for another three weeks to other towns in the South Island. After that I have a couple of weeks off, and, if you'd like to, I'll arrange a long horse trek.

"Our life in Boston will be very much as I told you. If you want to teach, that's fine. I'll share the housework. If you want to give the writing your best shot, I'll have the spare bedroom remodeled to give you your own study. Or if you want to be a homemaker, that's fine too.

"The choice is yours."

Judy sat a moment, mute. It had been a long speech, and the parts about the horse trek and the life in Boston were lovely. But overriding all this was the fact that it had been planned—planned between Jon and Dad and Mom. Her father directed and Jon wrote the script. She'd followed it as closely as if she'd studied the lines. She could control and orchestrate and teach a room full of thirty howling preteens, but to Dad and Jon she still couldn't take care of herself.

"Listen here, Jon Brown," she said finally, "you played with me. You manipulated me like a character in a book. Those comments about 'the script' weren't jokes or figures of speech. You wrote a plot, and put me into it."

He was actually nonplussed. *Good.*

"Judy," he said, "no—I mean, yes—but that's not

the way I meant it. I agreed to protect you, but then I fell in love with you. That's all."

Her voice trembled. "Yes, you love me. Dad and Mom love me, too. I'm twenty-five, I got straight As in school, and I'll bet none of the three of you could control mobs of adolescents the way I can, and I'm well on the way to writing a really good book. But what am I to you—to all of you? A little girl who needs to be taken care of. Sure, I had some environmental illness, but that was just a matter of time once I was away from the cause. But no, Daddy insisted on coddling me, and then you took over where Daddy left off."

She held her hands under the table so he couldn't see them shake. She could feel tears trembling on her eyelashes, and she swallowed hard and bit her lip. Jon Brown looked at her silently.

"I'm sorry," he said, somewhat formally, "I know you're a capable woman. You know the old saying about learning to swim by jumping off a dock. Now, you were doing the equivalent of starting by jumping from the high diving board into a damp rag. And I'd made promises to your parents.

"I'll try to do better in the future at treating you as an equal. Honest."

She hadn't even been in love with a man, she thought. She'd fallen in love with a character in a script. Jonathan Marlowe was an actor, and for her he'd played the part of plain Jon Brown.

But what a part it was.

She didn't love an academic or a scholar or a spin-

ner of plots. She loved plain Jon Brown, and plain Jon
Brown had taught her, by word if not by example, that
the truth was always best, and this professor, this cre-
ator of scripts and characters, was going to hear the
truth whether he liked it or not.

"Dr. J. Marlowe Brown," she said, "give me your
hand." She took his hand in both hers, and couldn't
resist running her thumb across the black hairs
springing from the backs of his fingers.

He smiled, once again very sure of himself.

"Now, Dr. Brown, I'm sure you're a very fine man,
and everyone I know speaks very highly of you, but
you are a stranger to me. The truth is, Dr. Brown, I'm
in love with someone else."

He looked at her in disbelief. "If you've made it up
with that—" he began, but she cut him off.

"No, it's not him. It's someone I met on this trip,"
she said.

"But you can't have?"

"Yes, I did, and I'm going to tell you about him.
Now shut up and listen. He's just a hick compared to
you. He's not well dressed, and at times his grammar
leaves something to be desired. But he loves me.

"He held me in his arms so I could sleep on the
plane. He cared for me after I almost had a car accident. And one rainy night, he slept on the ground in
front of my tent because he knew that I was frightened."

Her eyes misted over and a sharp lump grew in her
throat as she thought about it.

"I can't turn my back on that kind of love, Dr.

Brown, for all the famous novelists in the world. And besides all that, he drives me crazy. When he dances with me in the moonlight and when he kisses me, fireworks go off. He sings to me, and he calls me his sweetheart of the Bayside wharf.

"So, I'm sorry, Dr. Brown. This other man might be wild and crazy, and sometimes he embarrasses me, but he loves me, and I love him. He doesn't wear fake glasses. He abhors anything that isn't genuine, and he taught me to always tell the truth. And the truth is, Dr. Brown, that I want my rover not a scholar in a business suit. I want him, Dr. Brown, and I love him, and he loves me, so much. It took me a long time to realize how much. I want to marry *him*."

Both his hands gripped hers. He said gently, "You weren't supposed to know about the night in front of the tent."

"I know, but I couldn't sleep."

He squeezed her hands, and his blue eyes burned, almost like Jon's eyes. "I'm sorry you couldn't accept my proposal, Miss Gallant, but after hearing such a beautiful story, the only decent thing I can do is try to find the man you love. Now don't go away. Give me five minutes. Ten at the outside."

She watched him stride off. She tried to nibble at the seafood casserole which had grown cold while they talked, but she wasn't hungry. Jon hadn't touched his either.

Then he was back, dressed in his cutoffs and wearing the old hat over rumpled curls. He was carrying his guitar. She wanted to rush to him, but she couldn't move. Before she knew it, he was down on one knee before her, fingering the guitar and singing.

"I wooed you in Auckland. May I wed you in
    Christchurch?
"I wooed you in Auckland. May I wed you in
    Christchurch?
I've chased you all over this New Zealand coast,
I loved you in Bayside, I adored you in Queenstown,
But if you'll promise to wed me, I'll love you the
    most."

Their fellow diners weren't prepared for this. Besides, many of them were Jon's friends and colleagues. They broke into applause. Judy took the guitar from Jon and placed it on an empty chair. Then she pulled him to his feet and went into his arms.

"Yes," she whispered. "Yes, oh yes."

He kissed her to the accompaniment of further clapping and cheering. Then he said, "And now, my lovely, as we've made a spectacle of ourselves in front of all these people, and they're obviously expecting something, may I announce our engagement?"

She nodded, as she stood in her silk dress, pressed against his knit cotton shirt and worn cutoffs.

There was prolonged applause when he made the announcement, and a chorus of "Good on ya" came from both Jon's friends and total strangers.

Jon looked down at Judy. "Would you like your folks here? Do this up right."

She nodded.

"Mine, too," he said. "I'll phone them a bit later. It'll probably be a couple weeks before we can get everything together."

His lips brushed her hair. "Marlowe will go out to work each morning, and you'll have to tolerate him, fake glasses and all, at the occasional dinner party and social gathering, but it will be plain Jon Brown that comes home to you at night. Just in case you're worried, Jon is the real person and Marlowe is the fake, the act that pays the bills."

He gave her shoulder a little squeeze. "So have you got the feller you wanted?"

"Oh, yes," she said. Her eyes danced with mischief as she added, "but if you want to borrow one of Marlowe's suits for the wedding, I can handle it."

"Don't worry, darlin'," he assured her. "I won't embarrass you."

He picked up the guitar and began to sing. Within seconds, it seemed that everyone sang with him.

"I wooed her in Auckland. I'll wed her in
  Christchurch
I've chased her all over the from the East to the
  West.
I've loved her in campgrounds. I've loved her in the
  airports,
But when she stands at the altar, I'll love her the
  best."